Miracle Medics

Now celebrating its fifteenth anniversary,
Dr. David Kennedy's GDK Foundation organizes
a classic car rally through the UK countryside to
raise funds and awareness for transplant surgeries.
It will also give David a chance to
spend some quality time with his adopted son,
Dr. Josh Kennedy, a transplant specialist,
as they work together as navigator and driver.
Or, at least, that *was* the plan…

See classic cars and hearts sent racing as these
medics prove miracles are possible in:

How to Heal the Surgeon's Heart
By Ann McIntosh

As the charity road rally gets underway,
is it the race that has foundation founder
Dr. David Kennedy's heart pounding for the
first time in forever…or is it transplant recipient
coordinator Valerie Sterling?

Risking It All for a Second Chance
By Annie Claydon

When Josh and his ex, Dr. Emma Owen, are forced
to team up to complete the rally, tensions are high
in the confined space of her classic Mini Cooper.
Will the biggest hazard they face be the temptation
to start right where they left off?

Dear Reader,

This book was so much fun to write! Not just because of the wonderful Ann McIntosh, who wrote the first story in this duo, or the fabulous editors who worked on our stories with us, who together made writing this book an absolute joy. But also because I got to combine two elements close to my heart in the story: a second chance along with a tour around the towns and countryside of England and Wales.

Josh and Emma have already come to the conclusion that rekindling their disastrous love affair would be unthinkable, but when they have to join forces to finish the GDK Foundation's classic car rally, they can no longer avoid each other. There are so many reasons why this second chance may fail, but as there's the slightest chance that it may not they both have to take the risk. I found myself cheering for them all the way!

Thank you for reading Josh and Emma's story. I hope you enjoy it.

Annie x

RISKING IT ALL FOR A SECOND CHANCE

ANNIE CLAYDON

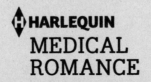

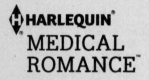

HARLEQUIN®
MEDICAL
ROMANCE™

Recycling programs
for this product may
not exist in your area.

ISBN-13: 978-1-335-40906-5

Risking It All for a Second Chance

Copyright © 2022 by Annie Claydon

This edition published by arrangement with Harlequin Books S.A.

For questions and comments about the quality of this book,
please contact us at CustomerService@Harlequin.com.

Harlequin Enterprises ULC
22 Adelaide St. West, 41st Floor
Toronto, Ontario M5H 4E3, Canada
www.Harlequin.com

Printed in U.S.A.

Cursed with a poor sense of direction and a propensity to read, **Annie Claydon** spent much of her childhood lost in books. A degree in English literature followed by a career in computing didn't lead directly to her perfect job—writing romance for Harlequin—but she has no regrets in taking the scenic route. She lives in London: a city where getting lost can be a joy.

Books by Annie Claydon

Harlequin Medical Romance

Dolphin Cove Vets
Healing the Vet's Heart

London Heroes
Falling for Her Italian Billionaire
Second Chance with the Single Mom

Best Friend to Royal Bride
Winning the Surgeon's Heart
A Rival to Steal Her Heart
The Best Man and the Bridesmaid
Greek Island Fling to Forever
Falling for the Brooding Doc
The Doctor's Reunion to Remember

Visit the Author Profile page
at Harlequin.com for more titles.

To Ann and Charlotte, with grateful thanks for nudges to the steering wheel when I needed them!

CHAPTER ONE

EVERYTHING HAD BEEN going so well.

Dr Emma Owen and her driving partner, Nurse Val Sterling, had reached the halfway point of the GDK Foundation's classic car rally. Emma's shiny nineteen-sixties Mini had taken them south from Edinburgh in a snaking route that went through countryside and cities. The foundation's events, held along the way to promote awareness and encourage people to donate blood and consider signing up to the various organ donor registers, had been far more successful than anyone could have dreamed. Just one more week to go, and Val and Emma could collect the sponsorship money that had been promised for the foundation. Val had taken a few minutes out from navigating the route this morning to work out how much they'd be raising per mile, and Emma had let out of whoop of achievement, as if the money was already safely in the bank...

Planning ahead like that was always a recipe

for disaster. Because from there on in, everything had slowly gone pear-shaped.

The Mini's engine had cut out a couple of times during the drive, and as they crossed the finishing line in Birmingham it had started to sputter again. Emma had pulled to one side and stopped, releasing the catch to open the bonnet. A local TV news crew who were covering the rally had zoned in on her and she'd waved them away crossly. Then all of Emma's attention had been diverted to Val, who had tripped over a trailing cable and hit the ground with a sickening thump, knocking herself out cold for a few seconds.

An ambulance had been called and the crew had agreed with Emma's assessment of the situation. Val expressed the expected outrage at being mollycoddled, but still, she sank back onto the ambulance gurney with an expression of relief. Emma left her car keys with one of the stewards, so they could move the Mini out of the way, and climbed into the back of the ambulance, ignoring Val's protests and taking her hand.

She left the hospital three hours later. Val was being kept in overnight for tests, and had already decided that she'd be fine after a little rest and promised to be back before the rally set off again from Birmingham. Emma had kept her doubts to herself, telling her friend that everything would be okay and she could find another navigator easily if Val needed a few more days' rest.

Things didn't improve from there. She found the Mini in a service bay, away from the other cars that stood beneath the fluttering banners that announced the foundation's rally and awareness event. Emma got in and tried to start it and the engine choked into life and then died again.

'Hi, Emma. You've just got back?' George Evans was standing by the car, his hands in the pockets of his overalls. He had the grace not to ask how things were going—the noise from the engine made that pretty obvious.

'Yes. Val's staying in hospital overnight but she should be back tomorrow.'

George nodded, scratching his head. He and his wife, Tess, had been retired for five years and had spent that time doing all the things they'd wanted to do but never got the chance. George was a car enthusiast, and his putting his aqua-blue 1946 Alpha Romeo through its paces was his main reason for joining the rally, although Tess's appetite for any good cause had added to their enthusiasm. They'd quickly become the rally's go-to couple if anyone wanted advice on mechanics or anything else.

'You think she'll be okay to continue?'

Emma shrugged. 'I'll be giving her the once-over when she gets back whether she likes it or not. I'm not going to allow Val to spend all day in the car navigating, if she's already got aches and pains.'

'What'll you do for a navigator?'

Emma could think about that when the time came. 'I might not need one. I have to see if I can get the car repaired first. It might be a blocked fuel line; I'll see if I can get it fixed tonight.'

George pursed his lips. He knew as well as Emma did that how easy the fix was going to be rather depended on where the blockage was.

'Why don't you go back to the hotel and check in? Get yourself something to eat and a good night's sleep. I'll be here first thing and give you a hand, eh?'

Emma swallowed down the impulse to shake her head and say that she could fix the car herself, tonight. George was far too good a mechanic to believe that and he didn't treat Emma as if she didn't know one end of a spanner from the other, like many of the men here did.

'Thanks, George. You're right, as always.'

'Off with you, then. Everything will look better in the morning.'

Everything *did* look a little better. The Birmingham awareness event would be starting at nine o'clock and there was a bustle of activity around the cars, which were lined up and newly polished, and in the booths where GDK staff were getting the information packs and donor cards ready. The blood donor mobile unit stood at the far end of the open space, along with a couple of smaller vans where green-uniformed NHS staff were setting up their information stand.

George and Tess were sitting on camping chairs, next to the Mini. Two grey heads, tilted towards each other because they still had something to say, even after forty years.

'Emma…!' Tess waved, bending to pick up the thermos at her feet. 'I've got some tea.'

'Can we save that for later, love?' George gave her a smile. 'We'll be needing to get started…'

The call came at lunchtime. Val was back at their hotel and feeling fine. But she'd just heard from the hospital where she and Emma worked and been told that a donor had been found for a seriously ill patient. As transplant co-ordinator, Val really should be there, but how was Emma going to manage without her?'

'Don't worry about things here. You go; the transplant is far more important. You're sure that you're all right?'

Val assured her that she was, and that the tests had given her a clean bill of health. She apologised a couple of times more and Emma told her that she had someone lined up already who would be able to navigate for her tomorrow, injecting an optimism into her tone that she didn't feel. She told Val she'd catch up with her when she got back to Liverpool, and they'd drink to the success of the rally, and the good health of Val's transplant patient.

'You've found someone?' Tess had returned with sandwiches and more tea, and was staring at her as she ended the call.

'No, but Val's needed in Liverpool. She and David are working with a patient who's been waiting for a kidney and pancreas transplant and now that a donor's been found Val has to go. I don't want her to feel guilty about leaving.'

'What about you?' Tess asked.

'I'm not involved with this particular case. I specialise in managing diseases of the liver. I'll be staying to finish the rally.'

Tess frowned. 'Well, you should have a cup of tea and something to eat. George can repair the car while you go and find a navigator—' She fell silent as George shook his head.

He knew. As they'd worked, Emma had told George that this was her dad's car. That she'd been 'helping' him service the engine since she was so small that she had to climb up on the bumper to see what he was doing, and that when she was sixteen she'd sketched out the design for the gold sunburst pattern around the back wheel arches. After Emma had left home for medical school, Dad had waited for her to visit before he took the engine apart, and they'd worked together on the Mini until he became too ill to go out into the garage. A year after his death, this rally was just as much about her dad, and how he'd have cheered the Mini across the finishing line, as it was about the cause she felt so strongly about.

'It's Emma's car, love. We've cleaned out the fuel transmission lines and it's just a matter of putting everything back together now. We'll let Emma do that while we ask round for a navigator.'

'Do you mind?' Emma shot George a grateful smile.

''Course not.' George started to unbutton his overalls. 'We'll have a cup of tea and then Tess and I will go and see what we can do.'

Emma had refitted the fuel line that ran under the car, which was the hardest part, and now she just had to connect the flexible hose that ran into the carburettor. George and Tess weren't back yet, and she knew they were probably having less success in their endeavour. The thought of having to give the rally up now was crushing.

One thing at a time. Emma bent over the engine, reaching over to position the hose, and felt something brush against the back of her knee.

She jumped, looking down into a pair of brown eyes, which were accompanied by one ear up and one ear down, along with a mottled black and brown coat and a wagging tail.

'Griff...!' Emma's voice splintered into an embarrassing squeak, as her throat dried and she noticed the feet planted next to him.

Griff wasn't the problem and nor was his usual companion, David Kennedy, the CEO of the GDK Foundation. But she'd heard that David had been called away to London last night, and clearly his son was filling in for him. Josh Kennedy, temporary dog-minder, transplant surgeon and, in David's absence, rally organiser. None of those job titles were particularly confronting; it was the ex-lover part that was making Emma's heart thump wildly.

She'd met Josh three years ago, through David. Emma had gone to the GDK Foundation to ask for help with a patient, and in addition to giving her some very solid advice, David had introduced Emma to his son. There had been a thrilling, world-turning affair that had lasted three months, and then it had all ended badly. So badly that Emma had thought twice about participating in the rally, but she'd wanted to come and reckoned that it would be easy enough to avoid Josh.

That had worked for the last week. It hadn't been so difficult because he'd obviously been avoiding her as well, and on the occasions when Emma hadn't seen him coming he'd been the one to swerve suddenly away. That unspoken agreement was clearly off the table and right now it felt that fate had saved its most uncomfortable blow, for last.

But there was nothing she could do about it. Emma dragged her gaze from his green and white sneakers and looked up at him.

'Hi, Emma. I heard that Val's out of the hospital. Is she okay?'

Okay. At least his first question wasn't an indignant enquiry about where the blazes she'd disappeared off to, three years ago…

'Yes. I spoke to her a little while ago and she's fine.'

Just as Emma was beginning to think that things couldn't get any worse, he smiled. That blue-eyed grin was all warmth and mischief, wrapped up in one gorgeous bundle.

'I'm glad to hear it. Fuel line problems?'

Since she was holding part of the Mini's fuel line in her hand, it wasn't exactly a stroke of diagnostic genius. 'Um…yes. I think so. Dad and I have had to unblock it before.'

Josh nodded. 'I was sorry to hear about your father's death. How's your mum doing?'

Her parents had liked Josh. Dad had involved him in a two-hour conversation which ranged from medicine to archaeology to the difficulty in getting spare parts for a classic car, and then nudged Emma and whispered to her not to let this one get away. Then she'd been the one to do the running...

'As well as can be expected, I guess. It was the first anniversary of Dad's death last month and that was hard for her, but she's keeping busy as usual.' Emma turned away from him quickly. The warmth in Josh's tone made her want to cry.

Fiddling with the fuel line was a good way of not looking at Josh. Maybe he'd just come to ask about Val and when he saw she was busy he'd leave her alone. But he didn't move, even though Griff was capering around in circles at the end of the lead.

'I...um...wanted to ask you something.'

His tone indicated that whatever it was, Emma wasn't going to like it. In David's absence for the day, Josh was clearly taking his second-in-command duties seriously and he had an annoying habit of wanting to plan everything down to the last excruciating detail. Emma straightened up.

'You heard that my father was in London last night, at an emergency board meeting?'

Curiosity got the better of Emma and she couldn't help asking even if it did threaten to prolong the conversation. 'I knew he wasn't here. There's been a problem?'

'There were some allegations about irregularities in the way the rally's been organised. He's succeeded in putting them to bed.' Josh shrugged. Clearly that was all sorted now, and wasn't his point. 'I've just heard from him; he was on his way back here, but he's been diverted to Liverpool.'

'Yes, Val's...' Emma bit her tongue. If Josh was in the same position she was, then it was better not to mention that she was in need of a navigator. 'I heard that they've found a donor for the kidney and pancreas transplant that David was supervising. That's good news.'

'Yes. Although it means I'm on the lookout for a driver so I can finish the rally. And I gather that Val's gone back to Liverpool as well.'

Emma froze, as the unthinkable presented itself as the obvious solution.

'Yes, that's right. George and Tess are finding me a replacement right now.'

At least she hoped they were. A whole week, in a Mini, with your ex. It didn't bear thinking about. And she was sure that Josh would be able to find a partner for the Daimler. Who wouldn't want to ride round in luxury with him as the perfect travelling companion?

'I just spoke with George and Tess. They're not having any luck. I was wondering if you'd like to join me and we can both finish the rally in the Daimler. It's comfortable and you could take your choice of either driving or navigating. I can have your name put on the car's insurance policy.'

'No!' At least she had the words she needed to reject *that* proposal. 'This car's started the rally and it's going to finish.'

'For your dad?' Josh instantly put his finger on the reason.

'Yes. For my dad. I'm sure you'll find some-one else.'

He nodded quietly, pushing his corn-blond hair back from his brow, in the way he always did when thinking around a problem. 'Or we could do things the easy way. I can navigate for you in the Mini. That way we'll both be able to finish and collect all the sponsorship money we have promised.'

'There's not much room.' It was all she could think of to say, other than, *Have you considered the possibility that we'll be at each other's throats before lunchtime?*

'We could try it out.' Josh shrugged. 'For the sake of the sponsorships…'

It went against the grain to be the inflexi-ble one, because that was Josh's speciality. She waved him towards the car and he pulled the front seat forward, letting Griff sprawl across the back seat. Then he got into the passenger seat. His long legs were bent uncomfortably and

Emma gave in to the obvious. 'You could push the seat back a bit. The lever's—'

Josh was already reaching for the lever under the seat. He pushed it back as far as it would go and Griff shifted a bit, then lunged forward, resting his head on Josh's shoulder. Josh chuckled, his long fingers caressing the dog's ears.

'Not so bad. We'll manage.'

His knees were no longer rammed up against the dashboard and if he kept his elbows to himself, then he wouldn't be getting in the way. Emma sighed.

'Do you have a restraint for Griff?'

'Yeah, and there's an attachment to his car harness that fits into a seat belt clip.'

Emma nodded. The seat belts in the car were the only thing that wasn't completely authentic. The Mini had been their family car and Dad had never compromised on safety.

'I've got a blanket for him as well, so he doesn't get dog hairs all over your seats. Dad seemed to think that it would be a familiar scent for him and calm him down.' Josh's fingers strayed to the dog's muzzle. It appeared that the one thing that calmed Griff was human contact, and he'd get plenty of that in the cramped confines of the Mini.

'I suppose... All right, then. We'll try it out for the run to Hay-on-Wye tomorrow and see how

it goes. If I can get the engine running, that is.'
Josh loved the security of a definite plan. The
uncertainty would at least concentrate his mind
a bit in looking for viable alternatives.

Josh got out of the car, and Griff bounded up
to her wagging his tail, as if he knew that they
were going to be teammates and he was determined to play his part.

'Thank you.' His lips twitched. 'I won't be
bringing any elephants with me. There isn't the
space.'

That was Josh all over. The smile, the charm.
The acknowledgement that they did have a history, but that he could ignore the elephants in the
room if she could.

'Yes, it would make things a bit cramped.'
Emma turned, trying to keep her face straight.
At this rate, the biggest hazard of driving with
Josh wasn't that they might be at each other's
throats. The temptation to connect with him on
a far more intimate level was making her heart
thump.

She could deal with that tomorrow. When she'd
got the Mini running.

'I'd better get on.'

'Would you like a hand? Griff and I are both
pretty enthusiastic assistants...'

Yeah, right. Blame the dog. Josh knew as much
about cars as she did.

'Thanks, I'm fine. George has been helping me and this bit's a one-person job. I'll text you and let you know whether this works and I get the car running.'

Admitting that she still had his number stored in her phone wasn't so terrible, but it was embarrassing that she *knew* that it was still there without looking. It was doubtful that Josh's quick perceptiveness had missed the faux pas, but he didn't comment on it. That was a start, at least.

'Great, thanks. If I don't hear from you I'll give you a call.'

He led Griff away, leaving Emma to turn back towards the car. Trying to ignore the thought that was throbbing in her head, now.

Josh still had *her* number too.

Emma still had her fire. Of course she did, it was something that wouldn't—couldn't—ever be contained. Her red hair was neatly tied back, the plait tucked down the back of her overalls, but Josh knew how it shimmered when spread loose across a pillow. He was just trying very hard not to think about it.

She would have had every right to tell him no, and to maintain the radio silence they'd been keeping for the first week of the rally. If he'd been asked his opinion, he would have said that was the thing to do and damn the consequences.

But he'd had no choice but to ask, both for the sake of the sponsorships and because the rally needed as many cars as possible taking part. And it seemed that Emma had felt she had no choice but to say yes.

'We'd better be on our best behaviour, eh, Griff?' At the sound of his name, Griff looked up at Josh, his one-ear-up-one-ear-down making it look as if he was querying him.

'Yeah, okay. *I'll* be on my best behaviour. You'll be fine.' Griff's tendency to do just as he pleased, whenever he pleased, would match Emma's view on life perfectly. It was Josh who had to show her that he could go with the flow.

As David Kennedy's adopted son, Josh had been given all the benefits of that—a good education and plenty of opportunities. David was his father in every possible sense of the word except one, and that was the one that mattered least to Josh. His biological father was just someone that his mother had known before David, and who Josh hadn't known at all.

He'd felt the consequences of his actions though. His biological father had kicked his mother and Josh out when Josh was just a baby. They'd had nothing, and his mother had been afraid to ask for help, in case Josh was taken away from her. For ten years the two of them had scraped to make ends meet, moving between squats and temporary housing until Josh hardly knew which way was home. David had fallen in love with Josh's mother's bright and unquenchable habit of making the best of things, and Josh had added his own surly disobedience to the mix. Why bother to fit in with David when they'd be moving on soon?

But they hadn't moved on. David and Georgie had got married and they'd formed a small, blended family of three. Josh had never had anyone he could call 'Gran' before, and David's mother didn't fit any of his expectations. A Black American woman with the cut-glass English accent of her adopted home, who brought with her a waft of expensive perfume, a shower of affection for her new daughter-in-law and grandson and fascinating stories about her travels whenever she arrived on their doorstep. He'd never had anyone he could call 'Dad' before either and having a father who actually knew who he was, let alone took any interest in him, was a novelty that Josh didn't always appreciate as much as his glamorous grandmother. But it didn't escape his notice that his mother was happy, and Georgie's imaginative charm had blossomed to fill every corner of their lives.

David had been the quiet, unassuming glue who held it all together. He'd adopted Josh, and patiently set about giving him a stable, secure home. And despite his unspoken rule of never really trusting anyone other than his mother, Josh had started to love him. When his mother had died suddenly when he was a teen, Josh had run away, reckoning that it would save David the trouble of handing him over to social services. But David had come for him and taken him home, telling him there was no place Josh could go that he wouldn't find him. It was tough love. Josh had been grounded for a month and told that he was expected to help out with David's latest project in the garden. David had been there, working with him and talking to him the whole time.

Emma had seen the man that David Kennedy had helped make, which was fair enough because Josh never talked about the frightened boy. When things had started to get serious with Emma, Josh knew he had come on too strong. Her carefree love of life had reminded him so much of his mother's, and Josh had reacted without thinking and changed his whole approach to the relationship. He'd always reckoned that he would give his own children the stable upbringing that he hadn't had for the first ten years of his life, and he'd responded badly to anything that Emma said or did which felt like a threat to the secure home he wanted to build with her.

So she'd done the only thing possible. The only

sensible thing to do in the circumstances. She'd run. Josh had been heartbroken, and known he'd been at fault. But he'd never called to explain, or tried to make things right. He'd coped the way he always had with loss, turning his back on it and pretending it had never happened.

But now, it looked as if Emma was agreeing to putting the past behind them. Forgetting was out of the question—Josh would be the first to caution her against that—but forgiving... No, that was probably out of the question too. But one man and his dog were a sufficient number of passengers in a Mini, and from the involuntary twitch of Emma's lips when he'd mentioned the elephants, it appeared that she too felt that it was best to leave them behind.

CHAPTER TWO

EMMA WAS BUSY counting her blessings. She'd been up early, fidgeting nervously as the race mechanic checked the repairs on her car. He'd passed the Mini as roadworthy, and the pre-dawn chill was beginning to give way to what promised to be a fine, clear morning... Those two would have to do.

Getting dressed for the rally wasn't as much fun as it had been last week. Not all of the rally teams were matching their costumes to the date of their cars, but she and Val had thrown themselves into the idea with enthusiasm, and they'd swapped accessories, done each other's hair and egged each other on to try out different make-up styles. But now her green minidress felt agonisingly short, instead of just a bit of fun, and the purple sparkly star on her cheek too frivolous. Her hair had refused to curl and the 'peace' sign on the pendant around her neck seemed like an impossible ambition for a day that would be spent with Josh.

She packed her luggage into the boot of the car and arrived late to the briefing for the day's driving. Josh was sitting in one of the front seats, already leafing through the information pack for the day. The route that the cars would take was carefully mapped out, and checkpoints along the way had to be noted in the navigator's log. There were some fun tasks to complete, and the cars had to conform to a strict speed limit—anyone who drove too fast over any part of the route would lose points.

Emma stood with a couple of the other drivers, at the back of the room. It was up to Josh to make sure they completed the course correctly; her job was to drive. The thought didn't fill her with as much excited anticipation as it had last week when Val had been her travel companion. Josh would undoubtedly stick to the plan, because making plans was what he excelled at. That wasn't such a bad thing in this context, but it brought with it the taste of sadness and anger, because it was what had broken them apart.

He was the same man that she'd fallen in love with, and it would be so easy to do it again. But from the moment they'd foolishly whispered those words to each other, wrapped up in the moment, Josh had changed. He'd started to talk about security and stability, mapping their lives out as if what they'd be doing in twenty years' time was an urgent decision that had to be made today. His easy-going nature had disappeared and life had become one big flow chart, with every possibility mapped out and recorded. It had become difficult to breathe, and Emma had known that if she didn't leave now, she never would.

It had taken a long time before she'd wanted to be anywhere other than in Josh's arms. Slowly she'd started to look forward, and then her world had stopped again when her father had been diagnosed with terminal cancer. She'd taken a job close to her parents' home so that she could be there for both of them.

It had been a long and painful year. Her plans for the future, which she'd always shared with her father with such joy, suddenly seemed hollow and meaningless, and when he'd died Emma had felt immobilised with grief.

But her mother no longer needed Emma's daily companionship. And Dad had always told her to keep her wheels turning. That was why she was here on the rally—in the hopes that something that would have given him joy would give her back her sense of moving forward in the world. And the one person who could shatter that fragile sense of new momentum was Josh.

As soon as the briefing was finished, Emma slipped away, ignoring the pairs of drivers and navigators who were looking through the information packs together. Josh would already be forming a clear idea of what came next and Emma had very little to add to that. Driving with Val had been teamwork, but this would be more a matter of listening to Josh's instructions and getting through the day.

She walked back to the Mini, then drove it to its place in the queue of nearly forty cars that would be checked out by the stewards at one-minute intervals when the rally got under way. Right on cue, not too early and not too late, she saw Josh walking towards her.

'You look great.' He was smiling and she saw Griff was dressed for the occasion, with a flowery patterned kerchief wound around his collar. Josh looked...

Gorgeous, as always. Almost golden in the morning sun, with his long corn-blond hair and tanned skin. He was wearing a collarless shirt, with the sleeves rolled up, and a pair of battered jeans, with his green sneakers. Simple, and as much of a nod to the nineteen-sixties as could be expected on such short notice.

'You too.' Emma hoped her words sounded like a polite response rather than a compliment. 'That's *all* of your luggage?' She pointed to the small holdall he was carrying, a rolled-up dog blanket stuffed between the handles.

Josh nodded. 'I reckoned there wouldn't be too

much space, and the only part of the nineteen-thirties costume I could use was the shirts. So I packed the rest up and it's going back to Dad's place in Oxfordshire today, with the Daimler. Do you have room for this?'

Plenty of room. Emma had squashed her luggage into precisely half of the space available and Josh was clearly travelling much lighter than she was. He opened the boot, dropping the holdall inside, and then ducked into the Mini, spreading the blanket on the back seat, while Griff pulled on the extending lead, nuzzling at Emma's legs.

'What do you think, then, Griff? Not quite as much luxury as you're used to.' Emma bent down to stroke his head, and the dog started to lick her hand.

'He'll be fine. Won't you, mate?' It seemed that addressing Griff as a go-between suited them both. Josh held the passenger door open, pointing at the back seat. 'In you go, then, Griff.'

Griff looked at him amiably and then ignored him, in favour of sitting down at Emma's feet and raising one of his paws to her. Griff loved being with people and he'd already learned a couple of tricks that were bound to get him attention. Emma clasped her hands behind her back, trying not to encourage him too much.

'Griff!' Josh's voice was a little firmer, his ges-

ture towards the back seat a little more emphasised. 'Come along, it's time to get in the car.'

Nothing. Griff was looking up at her, his eyes
pleading for attention, but if Emma gave it she
was going to disrupt Josh's agenda. Then she
heard Josh sigh.

'Okay. Whatever...'

That wasn't fair. It was the Josh she'd first met,
comfortable in his skin, laid-back and able to go
with the flow. The one she'd fallen in love with.

Then he gave her the smile that had once made
a prisoner out of her heart.

Emma bent down, stroking Griff's odd ears,
trying to keep her thoughts away from how good
it felt to be in Josh's arms. She'd been there, done
that...all of it...and it hadn't worked out. That
should be enough to keep her mind focused on
the rally and not on Josh.

Griff nuzzled against her, uncomplicated and
undemanding, and when she stood up and walked
around to the driver's door, he followed her.
Emma got into the car, and Griff clambered over
her, scrambling onto the back seat. Josh leaned
in, grinning, to fix his harness into the seat belt
clip. The cars ahead of them in the queue were
moving forward, and he got into the passenger
seat, moving his arm quickly when the back of
Emma's hand grazed it as she reached for the
gear stick.

They were close. Intimate, even, in the confined space. The Mini was a great car, but it didn't have Tardis technology installed, and it could get a little crowded. It was feeling extremely crowded at the moment, but perhaps when they started driving she wouldn't feel so bad. Emma cranked the handle to wind the window down, so she could at least rest her elbow on the open frame.

'Which way are we heading?' She really should have taken a bit more interest in the briefing session this morning.

Josh consulted the map that was perched on his knees. 'First left past the starting line, and then straight on for about…half a mile, until you get to a roundabout.'

That would do for starters. 'And what's our first clue?'

Josh chuckled. '*Swings and Roundabouts.* I think that one's easy enough, we'll be going past a park.'

He had everything under control. Of course he did. Today would probably go without a hitch and be easy driving. Just as long as she kept her eye on the road and not her navigator.

The morning had gone smoothly. Josh had given her exact instructions in good time, and Griff had piled out of the car with them to have his photograph taken, posing next to Emma on a swing. Then on, through the outer suburbs of Birmingham, the route twisting through back roads until they reached the country roads that snaked south-west into Wales and towards Hay-on-Wye.

The clue for their lunch stop was easy and they drew up outside the Unicorn Pub, taking turns to pose under the sign for pictures. There was an enormous sign announcing their arrival, which had obviously attracted some attention because the car park was full of people who'd come to see the cars, and the stewards had to clear a path so that Emma could manoeuvre into a parking space.

Everything was ready for them, and a large, open-sided marquee had been set up in the garden, serving drinks and food. Almost as soon as Josh had got out of the car, stretching his legs and back, the production assistant from the film crew that was accompanying the rally's celebrity team beckoned him.

'No rest for the wicked.' Josh grinned and Emma tried not to blush. She knew exactly how wicked he could be. 'Do you mind looking after Griff? We have an interview organised, but I think he could do with some water—his bowl's in my bag.'

'That's fine, I'll sort it out.' Emma wasn't going to go into Josh's bag though; that felt a little too much as if they were friends. Griff accompanied her over to the marquee, obviously delighted to be surrounded by people, and wagging his tail furiously. A bowl of water was found for him and as he lapped it up enthusiastically Emma glanced across towards Josh.

He was looking relaxed and cheerful, sitting down in front of the camera with a woman in a GDK Foundation sweatshirt and an older man. Ryan Winterhauer, the news presenter, joined the group, and the buzz of conversation around Emma subsided as the production assistant called for quiet. Griff tugged at the lead, seeming to realise where everyone's attention was now centred, and Emma followed him to the circle of people who had gathered to watch.

Emma had spent a day with Ryan during the first week of the rally. He was a nice guy, and fiercely committed to the foundation's work, being a transplant recipient himself. She wondered how Ryan's nose for a human interest story might track with Josh's predilection for facts and figures.

'This is Ryan Winterhauer, on the eighth day of the GDK Foundation classic car rally. We had a great day in Birmingham yesterday, and…' Ryan turned to Josh. 'I hear we had a record number of people sign up for donor cards?'

Josh nodded. 'We did, and we'd like to thank everyone who did so.'

'Absolutely. Today, we're on our way to Hay-on-Wye and we've stopped for lunch at the Unicorn Pub. We have the landlord here to thank for a very warm welcome.' Ryan turned to the older man. 'Jim, I gather you've been collecting pledges all week from potential blood donors.'

'Yes, when David Kennedy approached me on behalf of the GDK Foundation, this seemed like a really good cause for us to support. We have a wall of hearts inside, where people can sign their names, and anyone who can show me their blood donor card gets a free drink.'

Ryan nodded. 'That's great. I've had a sneak preview of the wall of hearts and you've obviously been working hard to get all those names. This kind of support means a lot to you, doesn't it, Josh?'

Josh nodded. 'Absolutely. As a surgeon, I see every day why the generosity of blood donors is so crucially important. Jim's not just collecting names, he's saving lives.'

Nice. Jim was clearly pleased with the thought as well, because he nodded, beaming at Josh.

'And we have someone here with us who can tell us a bit more about why it's so important.' Ryan turned to the young woman sitting beside

Josh. 'Maya, you have a very rare blood group, I believe.'

Maya smiled nervously. 'Yes, that's right. My parents come from India...' She looked up at Josh, obviously a bit lost for words.

'Maya's blood group occurs in about one in every ten thousand people of Indian ancestry, and in only one in a million people of European ancestry. This is why we're trying to reach as many people as we can from many different ethnic groups, so that appropriate medical care is available to everyone on an equal basis.' Josh had the numbers at his fingertips and Maya nodded gratefully.

'You give blood, don't you, Maya?' Josh prompted.

'Yes, I do. And I'd like to appeal to everyone in the Asian community to consider donating blood as well. And everyone else, of course.'

Josh nodded. 'Absolutely. Maya's made an important point. Every donation is vitally important, whatever your background or blood type. But at the moment, in addition to people of Asian heritage, we're also particularly appealing for donors of African and Caribbean heritage to come forward.'

'And why's that?' Ryan asked Josh.

'Certain blood disorders such as sickle cell disease, which are treated by giving blood transfusions, are more often found in people of Black African and Caribbean heritage. That means that there's an increasing demand for subtypes such as Ro, which are also more commonly found within that group.'

Ryan nodded. 'And as we've already heard that this doesn't just apply to blood donations, it's true for organ and bone marrow transplants as well. Patients from minority ethnic backgrounds currently face a longer wait for a donor match, don't they, Josh?'

'On average, yes, and that's why we're looking to diversify the register and support alternative treatments to keep patients well while they're waiting for a match. As I'm sure you understand, Ryan, each case is unique.'

'I do indeed. Which brings me on to another question. I know that many people have the same experience as I had when I needed a new kidney, which was that my brother offered me the gift of one of his.'

Josh nodded. 'Yes, it's not uncommon for family members to donate kidneys to their loved ones, and it's also possible to donate a section of your liver. The liver possesses the capacity to regenerate; both the transplanted section and the remaining section will regrow to normal size.'

'Fascinating. And I think you have a personal understanding of some of the issues involved in finding a suitable donor, because you're adopted, aren't you, Josh?'

It was no secret. But the slight flicker at the side of Josh's jaw showed that this question had come as a surprise.

'Yes, that's right. But I have no need for a suitable donor. I'm more interested in my patients' needs.'

'Absolutely.' Ryan had found his human interest angle to the story and Josh's reticence was like a red rag to a bull. 'But I think that your situation is relevant to many people who *are* waiting for donations.'

'That's true. People like me, who are adopted, may also face difficulties in finding an organ match.'

'Is that because they aren't in touch with their real parents? You aren't, are you?'

Josh's lip curled slightly. So imperceptibly that you'd have to know him well to see it, and maybe Ryan didn't realise that he'd just touched on what seemed to be a very sore point for Josh.

'My mother died when I was sixteen. And my real father is David Kennedy.'

'Yes, of course.' Ryan had the grace to look a little chastened, but not so much that he was going to give up his line of questioning. 'But you're not in touch with your biological father?'

'No.'

Ryan nodded. 'That must feel…' He left the question open, clearly wanting Josh to fill in the gap.

This was too much. It wasn't relevant to the GDK Foundation's core message, which was to work to provide treatment for every patient. And it was perfectly clear to Emma that Josh didn't want to talk about this. Emma knew that Josh was adopted, and that he saw David as his true father, but Josh had never said a word about the circumstances of his adoption.

Griff had been pulling on the lead, and it was obvious what was on his mind. Emma let go of the lead and he galloped over to Ryan, putting his paws up onto his knees and making a lunge for the microphone. When Ryan jerked it out of his reach, Griff flung himself at Josh, in a frenzy of canine love. Josh laughed suddenly, and Maya leaned over to stroke Griff, who responded by nuzzling against her hand.

The moment of awkwardness was broken, and Ryan bowed to the inevitable. He made a joke about Griff being the rally's most enthusiastic competitor and then turned to Jim.

'I think now's the time to go and see your donor wall, if that's okay, Jim?'

'Of course.' Jim got to his feet quickly, clearly pleased to be able to show off his efforts, and

Ryan beckoned to the camera and followed him inside the pub.

Josh was on his feet too, talking to Maya and shaking her hand. A man approached them, carrying a toddler, and it looked as if an introduction was being made, because Josh shook his hand as well. He stopped to talk for a few minutes and then bade them a cheery goodbye, walking back over to Emma.

He knew what she'd done. The look on his face was unmistakeable, and it was making her heart thump. An understanding that went beyond words and touched at the intimacy they'd once shared.

'Griff to the rescue.'

'Difficult to keep him under control, sometimes.'

Josh nodded, the warmth in his eyes reminding her of how he'd once looked at her. 'Yeah. You know the story of how Dad got to meet him?'

'No.' Whatever it was, it was obviously nothing to do with her relationship with Josh, which was a relief.

'He was appearing on a chat show, and the next guests were involved with an animal shelter and had brought some of the dogs along with them. Griff was one of them, and he managed to slip his leash and bounded out onto the set, wanting to make friends with Dad.' Josh laughed. 'My father doesn't like to make this known, but he's a really soft touch. He fell in love with Griff on the spot, and ended up taking him home with him.'

'So Griff's our press liaison officer, then?' Emma ventured jokingly.

'Yep. Seems he's a very good one.' Josh stroked Griff's head approvingly. 'Buy you lunch?'

He didn't need to. Emma would have done exactly the same thing for anyone who'd been put into the position that Josh had been in.

'That's okay. Jim's making no charge for the competitors' lunches.'

'That's generous. Can I *collect* your lunch, then? You go and find a seat, and—' Josh handed her Griff's lead '—keep a good hold on his lead this time.'

The mischief in Josh's grin was too hot to handle. Emma nodded, turning away to scan the pub garden for a couple of empty seats.

CHAPTER THREE

THIS WAS…EXCRUCIATING. Excruciatingly awkward at times, and Josh was having to keep on his toes to avoid the elephants that insisted on appearing around them. He'd reckoned that he could be an adult and keep his longing for Emma under control, but that was excruciatingly difficult at times too.

Her ebullient love of life was firmly subdued while she was in the car with him. But it popped to the surface like a cork when she got out, posing under signs and next to waypoints that were listed out in the day's route plan. Josh had taken photographs—because the rules demanded that photographic evidence should be submitted—but there were a lot more than strictly necessary on his phone. He hadn't been able to resist capturing just a little bit of everything he'd lost.

He hadn't been able to resist dwelling on their parting either. The way he'd changed, trying to reconcile his love for her with the fear that her free spirit would cause just as much havoc as his mother's had. Their last bitter argument had driven Emma away, but it wasn't that which had convinced him that there was no going back. It was his fear of loss, which had led him to obliterate her from his life, as if she'd never existed.

But the sight of Emma in a green minidress, her red hair backcombed and tucked into a ponytail, was pushing buttons that Josh didn't even know he had, and really didn't bear thinking about. He'd kept his eyes on the map and on the road ahead, and when they crossed the finishing line in Hay-on-Wye, he'd grabbed Griff's lead and taken himself off to present the stewards with the evidence that they'd completed the route correctly, while Emma took the car to find a parking spot. The awareness events for smaller towns were low-key and organised by local GDK Foundation representatives, and so Josh was able to escape to yet another hotel room, sitting down with Griff sprawled awkwardly across his legs, to check his email.

There were a few that had nothing to do with the rally, and a quick glance through them was enough to ignore them until later. One was from David, and was surprisingly jocular in tone, given the fact that he'd just had to abandon a rally that he'd worked hard to organise for over a year now. Josh replied to him quickly, telling him that everything was going swimmingly and not mentioning that he felt he might drown at any minute. That left the mass of emails from the other rally participants.

Social media really wasn't Josh's thing. Neither were blogs. But since the rally was all about awareness, the GDK Foundation had been making as much use as it could of both, and David had been uploading photographs from each day on the blog that the foundation's IT guru, Evie, had integrated into their website. Now that was Josh's job, and he decided that it needed yet another call to Evie.

'Hey, Evie, I'm really sorry about this...'

'No problem. IT questions are what I live for, and yours are always remarkably easy to answer.' Evie's voice floated across the ether. The idea that there was even such a thing as an easy-to-answer question right now lifted his mood.

'Have I mentioned that you're a star?'

'You did. A couple of times yesterday, actually.'

It had been well deserved. Evie had given up part of her evening to talk Josh through putting the photographs from the awareness event up onto the blog. At least he'd managed to phone during working hours this time, and if he kept it short he wouldn't be keeping her late at work.

'I'll think of some other flattering epithet for

tonight, then. You couldn't just run through how to set up a new blog post again, could you?'

'Of course. Are you sitting comfortably? Laptop at the ready?'

'Yep.'

Evie chuckled. 'Then I'll begin...'

Josh had cut his conversation with Evie short at precisely five thirty, so that she could go home on time, and then carefully consulted the notes he'd made, repeating the instructions until all of the photographs were up on the blog. When he previewed the post, it didn't have quite the effortless design style of David's posts, but then Josh hadn't had the advantage of regular lessons with Evie before the rally started.

It was good enough though, even if it didn't quite satisfy his surgeon's appreciation of precision. And it would have to do, because Griff was getting restive. This was a dog-friendly hotel, but they might object if Griff was howling all night, and if Josh didn't take him out to work off some of that excess energy, that might well be what happened.

He jogged with Griff down to the centre of the town. The book festival in Hay-on-Wye had finished a couple of weeks ago, but there were still lengths of bunting, fluttering in the breeze, and the bookshops, although closed, were good for a little window gazing. He had his hand cupped against a glass shop front, so he could see some of the titles at the back of the display, when Emma's voice behind him made him jump.

'It doesn't look as if Griff shares your interest in books.'

Josh turned, and in the split second that he allowed himself to look at Emma, he was rewarded with the sight of her in blue jeans and a cosy jacket, her red hair loose around her shoulders and glinting in the evening sun. Then he looked down at Griff, who was busy gnawing at a Victorian boot-scraper beside the entrance of the shop.

'Griff! Stop that!' He rolled his eyes. 'I swear, the first thing I do when I get back to London is to sign my dad and Griff up for some obedience classes.'

Emma grinned suddenly. 'Obedience classes for David, you mean? Griff's a bit wayward but that's what everyone seems to love about him.'

She'd caught him with his hang-ups showing again. There was nothing wrong with Griff's free spirit, although it might be nice if he actually came when you called him.

'Since the relationship between my dad and his dog *is* largely Dad doing what Griff tells him, then that's probably going to be the way forward. I can think of worse solutions.'

Emma nodded. 'Yes, me too.'

This was nice. Together in the cool of the evening, with enough room to give each other a little space and maybe talk a bit. 'Which way are you walking?'

'That way.' Emma pointed along the high street. 'I thought I might stroll past a few bookshops and look in the windows.'

Just as he'd been doing. 'May I join you?'

'Yes, of course.' Emma started to walk, keeping Griff in between them. But she hadn't hesitated in agreeing, so in the absence of evidence to the contrary, Josh was going to take that as an indication that they might learn to be a bit less stiff in each other's company.

They walked slowly along the high street, their breath misting the glass as they peered through the windows of second-hand bookshops. Griff began to join in, standing on his hind legs to see the irregular rows of books, their spines faded with age. Emma looked down at him, smiling and ruffling his ears.

'Your father always seems so reserved and businesslike at work. Griff shows him in an entirely different light...' Emma tilted her head slightly, in an indication that this might be a question. Josh imagined that she meant it to be whatever he wanted it to be. She had clearly seen his discomfiture about the questions that Ryan had asked, because she'd enlisted Griff's help in doing something about it.

And he wanted to explain. If she knew that his behaviour during their short-lived love affair had been provoked by fear, then maybe they could be friends. Or at least slightly more comfortable as driver and navigator.

'Dad's got his soft side, even if he doesn't show it much. He has a way with waifs and strays…as I found out when I was a kid.'

'I'd always assumed that you were adopted as a baby. Not that you ever said.' Emma was interested now. He could see it in the way that she suddenly looked up at him. But she quickly looked away again, still refusing to ask an explicit question.

'No, Dad adopted me when I was eleven, when he married my mum. She was only sixteen when she had me, and her parents put a lot of pressure on her to marry my biological father. That fell apart pretty quickly and I never knew him.'

'So she brought you up on her own? Until she met David…' Finally Emma had asked an actual question. She obviously wanted to know, and maybe she needed to draw a line under the past as much as Josh did.

'Yeah. Although it seemed sometimes as if I was her travelling companion rather than her child. Mum was great. She loved me, and she had a knack of making the best of things.'

Emma thought for a moment, pursing her lips. And when she asked, warmth flooded through Josh. 'It sounds as if *things* needed to be made the best of?'

'She had nothing when my biological father kicked her out. We moved around, from squats to temporary accommodation, and I was at a whole succession of different schools.' He shrugged. 'I never had the right uniform.'

That had been one of the preoccupations of his young life. Not where the next meal was coming from, because somehow his mother always kept his stomach full, even if she didn't eat herself. Not toys or games, or whether he had his own bedroom, because they were transient things anyway and he'd been used to not getting too attached. But having the right school uniform had meant that he could at least pretend to fit in with the other kids.

And Emma seemed to understand, nodding gravely. 'We moved around a lot for my dad's job when I was little. As he was an archaeologist we went where the digs were. But it was different for me. Mum and Dad always gave me a sense of security and belonging. It was just the things around me that were changing.'

'The first person I really felt I belonged with

was Dad. I'd been used to running wild before
we went to live with him, and it was a bit of a
shock to find that he had a set of rules.'

'I'll bet he did.' Emma chuckled. 'I wouldn't
like to be the one that broke David's rules.'

Josh laughed, the warm feeling of understanding and acceptance making him feel slightly
light-headed. 'No, I found that out very quickly.
It was hard, but he turned my life around. Mum
loved him to bits, and I learned to.'

'And then you lost your mother.' Emma was
grave again.

'Yeah. I didn't believe that David would want
me after that, and I couldn't bear to face another
loss, so I took matters into my own hands and
ran away. I didn't get very far, and he managed
to catch up with me.'

'And he was furious?'

'Incandescent, more like. He told me that
there was nowhere I could possibly go where
he wouldn't find me and bring me back. He
grounded me for a month and took time off work
and made me help him with the garden shed he'd
been meaning to build. I pretended to mind, but
I knew he was angry because he loved me. We
made a great job of the shed together as well.
Brick built, with a bow window that Dad had
hauled out of a skip.'

'David built a shed! With bricks…?'

'Yeah, he can do that kind of thing. He doesn't do it much now; the inheritance from his father, that he set the GDK Foundation up with, changed all that. But if you ever need any advice on shed-building he's your man.'

'Always good to know, I'll bear it in mind.' Emma grinned impishly. 'Does he do garages?'

'Dad's multi-talented, a garage is a piece of cake. Why, you're thinking of having one?' Josh couldn't quite see Emma wanting to build a garage. That implied ownership of property and the idea that she might settle down in one place at some point.

'No, not really. Just so I know who to ask if I ever do want one. It's best to keep an older car off the road.'

Maybe it was his imagination, but Emma seemed to be walking a little closer. Maybe she understood why he'd acted the way he had, and didn't blame him so much for it, now. But it seemed that would remain unsaid, as she turned to look into the next shop window.

They walked the length of the high street and then turned and strolled back to the hotel. Emma stopped just outside the entrance, saying she wanted to go and check on the Mini, before turning in for the night, making a fuss of Griff before they parted.

It hurt. More even than when they'd rowed

and Emma had stormed away from him, because then there had been no understanding, just hurt. It felt as if things had changed a lot in the last hour. But they probably hadn't changed so much for Emma, and Josh swallowed his feelings and bade her a goodnight.

'Josh…' They'd both turned to walk away, but Emma called him back. There was evidently one last thing she had to say, probably something about the rally.

'Yep?' His gaze met hers and suddenly the rally was the last thing in his thoughts.

'We're alike in a lot of ways but… I never realised just how different we are as well.'

He could almost hear the thunder of elephants stampeding over the horizon. And that was okay, because maybe they did need to talk about the one thing that had been on his mind almost constantly, and which seemed to have been on Emma's as well.

'Alike enough to be friends and different enough to make a real mess of a relationship?' Josh ventured the observation.

'Yes. That…' Emma shrugged, and Josh wondered if she regretted it as much as he did.

'It was my fault, Emma. I was a very insecure kid, and…' It was hard to admit even now. 'I don't talk about it and I've tried to put it all behind me. Sometimes I can't.'

Emma shrugged again. 'None of us can put those formative years completely behind us.'

It was time to apologise. It couldn't make things right, but it was the right thing to do. 'I'm sorry for what I said. About you being irresponsible...' And unable to settle. Childish, reckless, thoughtless...

'Consider it unsaid. I'm sorry for what I called you too.'

Stick-in-the-mud, joyless, unimaginative... That had really stung, even though Emma had added the caveat *outside the bedroom*. She'd always been fair-minded, even when she was ferociously angry.

'Consider that unsaid too. Although I think you may have been right. If we'd known then what we know now...'

They would have known they were incompatible and never would have considered a relationship. But despite all of the pain, it was something that Josh couldn't bring himself to wish away.

Emma nodded. 'We know it now. I guess I'll say goodnight, then.'

He didn't want her to go. He wanted to take her in his arms and tell her never to change because she was perfect just as she was. But they'd come to a fragile understanding, one that was very overdue, and Josh wouldn't risk damaging that.

'Yeah. Goodnight.'

CHAPTER FOUR

EMMA HAD BEEN up early, after a night spent thinking about things that hadn't been said and the differences between her and Josh. She'd come to no conclusion, apart from the fact that it was impossible to traverse a space which seemed to have no footholds.

She spent a little more time on her outfit, choosing a slim-fitting cheesecloth shirt and flared hipster jeans with a rainbow-coloured belt. Flat leather sandals and strings of beads around her neck completed the look, along with a small bell that jangled annoyingly every time she moved. Bells and beads were okay in theory, and definitely a sixties look, but how on earth did they put up with the constant noise?

Josh was already in the hotel lounge, which had been commandeered for the morning briefing. This time he sat alone, his copy of the day's information pack placed on the chair next to him. Saving her a seat was one thing, and a nice friendly thing to do, but did he *really* have to look at her with those come-to-bed eyes?

Emma reminded herself that he couldn't help it. She'd always liked Josh's eyes, and from the first moment they'd met they'd seemed to be beckoning to her. It was *her* appreciation of them that gave them the come-to-bed quality, and nothing that Josh did. She gave him a wave, squeezing past the people already seated in that row, and plumped herself down next to him.

'You're sitting on our information pack.' Josh gave her a simmering smile.

'Oh. Sorry.' Emma shifted, handing him the typed pages. Josh was clearly enlarging on the hippy theme he'd adopted yesterday, and had added a strip of fabric and a leather thong tied around his wrist. The splash of colour drew attention to his arms, which in general was a good look, but only made Emma think of the way he might be holding her while he gave her the come-to-bed look.

Enough! Today was all about the rally. If it also promised the possibility that they might be a little more friendly with each other, that should have nothing to do with Josh's allure. In fact, thinking about anything other than friendship was going to make said friendship out of the question.

'I've got something for you. To add to the look.' Emma took one of the bead bracelets from her own wrist and handed it to him, hoping he wouldn't take the gift the wrong way.

He looked at the black and grey beads, and the tiny 'peace' sign next to the clasp. The curve of his lips told her that he was taking this the right way.

'This is yours?'

Emma shook her head quickly. 'Val and I brought along a jar of beads and some bead wire, so we could make our own jewellery along the way. I made this for you. If you like it, that is…'

'Yes, I do. Thank you.' He fiddled with the clip, trying to fasten it, and Emma leaned forward, securing the beads around his wrist, next to the leather thong.

'Everybody…!' The race co-ordinator's voice sounded above the chatter and the room fell quiet. Emma breathed a sigh of relief. Now perhaps she could concentrate on what came next.

Everything about Emma was perfect. The way she looked and the things she did. Even the tiny 'peace' sign that was now hanging from his wrist. The beads had been a nice thought, but Emma never did anything without understanding its connotations. If she'd given him a 'peace' sign, then that was what she'd meant to say to him.

Today they'd be making the run into Cardiff, the second of the British capital cities that the rally was visiting. They squeezed into the Mini with just as much care as they'd done yesterday, but this morning felt a little different. The anger and resentment was gone—or at least well under wraps. When Emma reached for the gearstick and Josh moved his leg slightly so that the back of her hand wouldn't brush his thigh, it was more a matter of knowing that her touch had the power to spoil the fragile peace between them.

As they drove out of Hay-on-Wye, Emma wound down the car window, waving a joyful goodbye to the town. Josh smiled to himself, concentrating on giving her plain instructions in good time, and today they weren't met by silent compliance, but with a nod of the head and sometimes a few words. They were getting there, in more ways than one.

The distinctive, flat-topped outline of Crug Hywel rose on the horizon, and there was the obligatory picture of Emma, her arms above her head so it looked as if she was supporting the vast bulk of the mountain. Then back into the car again to follow the road, which alternated between the soft dappled sunlight of woodlands, and the wonderful views of the Brecon Beacons. Suddenly Emma pulled over to the side of the road.

'Straight on, here…' Straight on wasn't the best description of the twists and turns in the road, but since it was the only route available, Josh reckoned it was obvious. He turned to Emma questioningly.

'Yes, I know.' She grabbed at the beads around her neck, disentangling a small bell that hung amongst them. 'This bell's driving me nuts. I'm going to put it in the glove compartment.'

Josh chuckled. He'd been thinking that the bell was rather charming, and that Emma had hit on a sixties icon that everyone understood with her bells and beads. He supposed that if you were actually wearing the bell it might be a little less adorable.

'It's going to drive you nuts in the glove compartment; you'll be thinking that it's the engine rattling. Here, give it to me.' Josh peeled a piece of sticky tape from the vinyl cover of today's information pack, and Emma leaned forward, dropping the bell into his hand without taking the long chain from her neck. His hand shook a little at the unexpected intimacy of the move, but he managed to secure the sticky tape around the tiny striker of the bell.

'Better?'

Emma leaned back, rattling the beads together, and Josh heard no accompanying jingle from the bell. 'Ah, nice job. Thanks. Having a surgeon in the car does come in handy, after all.'

They seemed to be moving from silence,

through careful pleasantries and on to cheerful teasing. That had been the most delicate operation, and Josh was pleased it was going well.

'Let's get moving, then. We don't want to fall behind schedule.'

Emma shot him a grin and started the car. Climbing through woodlands, the road opened up again into a spectacular view of the mountains, and suddenly she turned off the road.

'Wait… This isn't right…' Josh looked up from the map as the car accelerated, bumping along an uneven track.

Then he saw it. It was nothing short of a miracle that Emma had noticed the flash of aqua blue from the road, as the Alpha Romeo was tucked into a fold in the landscape. But Josh could see it now, the driver's side of the bonnet crumpled against a large tree.

Emma slammed on the brakes and Griff complained momentarily from the back seat, before his head sank back down to rest sleepily on his paws. Emma was already out of the car, tucking the mass of beads into her shirt and buttoning it up as she went.

'Is that George and Tess?' Josh followed her.

'Yes.' Emma pulled the boot open, moving her own luggage out of the way so that she could reach a surprisingly bulky first aid kit. She handed it to Josh and they jogged together across the uneven ground.

As they got closer, Josh could see two grey heads, still in the car, and that the driver's side of the windscreen was smashed and buckled. George and Tess had been talking just the other day about how retirement seemed like one long holiday. It looked as if the holiday had just come to an abrupt end, and Josh hoped against hope that neither of them were too badly hurt.

'Tess… Tess…' Emma had run round to the passenger seat of the car, and Josh saw her lean in, and heard the sound of Tess crying. George seemed to be motionless in the driver's seat, and Josh made for him.

'He's bleeding, Emma… I can't stop the bleeding.'

Emma glanced up at Josh, who was carefully prising the driver's door open as far as it would go. George seemed to be unconscious and pinned to the front seat by a strut that had come loose from the side of the windscreen. There was blood everywhere.

'I've got George. Will you call for an ambulance?'

Emma pulled out her phone and dialled, tucking the phone between her chin and her shoulder as she opened the passenger door. Before she could stop her, Tess got out of the car, seemingly not badly injured, and Emma led her away, talking quickly on the phone. Josh turned his attention to George.

She'd clearly made the same assessment of the situation that he had, because Josh had barely located the source of the bleeding, tearing George's shirt to expose the wound, when Emma appeared again at the open passenger door.

'Airways are clear and he's unconscious.' Josh automatically reeled off his observations. 'One of the support struts for the windscreen has been driven right through his shoulder and is pinning him to the seat. I don't see any other bleeding.'

Emma nodded. Josh was about to ask her if she'd come around this side of the car and monitor George's wound, while he got inside to check on him, but she was already in the car, squeezing past the buckled dashboard to reach George.

'There's some gauze in the first aid kit. And gloves...'

This was probably the best use of their resources, but Josh didn't like it that Emma had crawled into the car, while he was safely outside. She'd done it now though, and he bent to open the box at his feet, keeping one hand on the wound to stem the bleeding and hooking out a packet of gauze with the other.

'How's his pulse?' Josh quickly packed the gauze around the wound.

'Steady. His breathing's okay.'

'Then let's keep him in situ for a moment while I take a look at the back of the seat to see if I can get the strut out if I need to.'

'All right.' Josh felt her hand on top of his, keeping the pressure up on the wound as he craned around. He could see the slender tip of the metal protruding from the back of the seat and it looked as if there was nothing that would prevent him from withdrawing the strut from the other side.

If he did that, then he could well damage an artery and George might bleed to death. He'd almost certainly do more damage to his shoulder than if the strut were removed in an operating theatre. But if George stopped breathing or his heart failed, they'd have to take those risks in order to get him out of the car and resuscitate him. Emma was closest to George and she could monitor him more thoroughly, which meant that the decision about whether it was safe to keep him in the car until the ambulance arrived was hers alone.

It was a huge weight of responsibility, and Josh had wanted to take that burden himself. But now there was no option, and he knew exactly what she needed. It was what he needed in the operating theatre: support and communication from the people around him.

'I can get him free and out of the car. It's on your word, Em. I need you to tell me if it looks as if he's in difficulties.'

She puffed out a breath, and then nodded. 'Okay. I'm going to get closer.'

Emma wriggled round, in a manoeuvre that Josh couldn't have managed in the confined space, carefully swinging so that she could directly face him. Josh used his free hand to steady her.

'Thanks. There's a stethoscope in my bag.'

Josh hooked the stethoscope out of her bag with one hand, putting it around her neck and positioning the diaphragm against George's chest. Emma clipped the earpieces into her ears, listening for a moment.

'Sounds good. Let me listen to his chest.'

Josh moved the diaphragm again, and Emma nodded. 'Good. Surprisingly so. We'll stay here.'

'Okay. The bleeding is stopping…' Now all they needed to do was to keep things that way, until help arrived. 'Did they say how long the ambulance would be?'

'About ten minutes. They're sending a fire and rescue truck as well. Should be here any time, now.'

'Good. Hang in there.'

She glanced up at him for one moment, but that was enough. Josh saw the motion of her lips, framing the words *Thank you*, and knew that Emma was relying on him.

They kept working. Checking and then checking again that George's vital signs were stable and that there was no internal bleeding. He saw Emma's smile when the sounds of sirens reached their ears, and popped his head out of the car for one moment, calling to Tess, who had jumped to her feet.

'Tess, please stay there. We're doing all we can for George and he's stable at the moment.'

That was all he could say in the way of reassurance right now, but in the few minutes she'd spent with her, Emma must have managed to impress on Tess that she could best help by staying out of the way. Tess sat back down, hugging her arms around her chest and rocking silently.

They kept working, and when the ambulance crew arrived, Josh ducked quickly out of the car to speak to them, telling them he was a doctor and showing them the ID in his wallet, then quickly relaying George's condition. He broke off, as he heard Emma call out to him.

'Josh... Help me, he's waking up.'

Josh returned to the car and dropped to one knee again. George was showing every sign of beginning to regain consciousness, and at any moment he would be in a lot of pain. The paramedic saw immediately what was needed and confirmed that he was carrying analgesic, and Josh agreed to the intended dose.

'I'm going to try to hold him still, but you need to talk to him, Em.' If anything could calm George it would be the sound of her voice.

It was a lot to ask, but Emma nodded. She leaned down, tapping the side of George's face with her finger as Josh braced his arms around his shoulder to keep it still. 'George. It's Emma. Listen to me, George…'

George was moaning now, and starting to move. 'George. It's Emma. Try to stay still for me.'

'Tess…' The one word sounded like a howl of pain.

'Tess is all right. She's fine, she's waiting for you, George. Stay still for me.'

Emma kept talking to him, as the paramedic squeezed alongside Josh, administering the shot. George was whimpering with pain, but he was listening to her and doing his best to keep still, which made it easier for Josh to hold his shoulder steady.

Emma had done it. Josh had been dreading what might happen when George woke up but she'd got them over that hurdle and the fast-acting analgesics would be kicking in soon. They still had a lot left to do, but they were a team now, thinking and acting as one. If anything could get George out in one piece, it was their teamwork.

Josh had been her strength. He'd been calm and supportive, helping her to monitor George and make the decisions that she needed to make. The analgesics were taking effect, and Emma was able to gauge George's condition better now using the ambulance equipment that Josh was handing in for her.

'Tess...' George's speech was beginning to slur.

'Tess is fine, George. She's got one of the ambulance crew with her, and they're looking after her.' Josh had been keeping her informed about what was going on outside the car as well.

'I have to see her.'

'I know, and you'll see her soon. There's a team working right now to get you out of the car. You've been so brave. I just need you to hold on a little bit longer.'

'I'll...try...' George's eyelids were beginning to droop and Emma gently tapped the side of his face to keep his attention. It was a delicate balance; George wouldn't feel any pain if he slipped back into unconsciousness, but it was important to keep him awake so that he was able to register any distress.

'Don't you wanna shout, *Stay with me*?' George's

dry sense of humour surfaced suddenly, probably encouraged by the level of opioids in his bloodstream.

'I could do. Best not to shout though, or Tess will hear me.'

'Uh.' George winced as another wave of pain gripped him. 'Yeah. Good girl.'

'The fire and rescue guys are ready. Want me to take over?' Josh's voice caught her attention.

Yes. Emma was scared and she wanted to stretch her cramped and aching limbs. But Josh couldn't get into this confined space and George was trusting her to stay with him.

'I'm fine. Tell them to get on with it.'

One moment. It was more than enough time to feel the warmth of his blue eyes washing over her. Comforting her and giving her strength. She'd seen the trace of concern in his face when she'd got into the car, and if Josh reckoned that her actions were irresponsible or reckless, he was keeping it to himself.

'Okay. The protective shield's on its way.'

She felt his fingers brush her arm as the firefighters moved in to tuck the flexible shields around her and George. Feeling Josh there made it easier to be strong for George, and she could tell him what he needed to hear quietly and confidently.

She heard the order to stand back, but knew

Josh was still there. She could hear his voice, and focusing on that made it easier to comfort George effectively.

The car vibrated as the fire and rescue team peeled its roof back, like the skin of an orange. George swore quietly, at the thought of his beloved Alpha being cut to bits, but Emma had already prepared him for it, and he knew it had to be done. More noise and vibration as the seat was freed from its housing, and then the protective shields were removed, and Emma blinked in the afternoon sun.

'Time to move, Em.' Josh was back again.

'Uh… Give me a moment.' She'd been crouched in the same position for so long now that it felt as if her arms and legs had locked into position.

'Relax. Let go.' Josh wrapped his arms around her, lifting her away from George. As he set her on her feet she felt his lips brush her cheek. Probably by accident.

No. Not by accident. There had been no room for error this afternoon and the look in Josh's eyes told her that this was no accident either. But he had to go now, and he turned away, helping the ambulance paramedic carefully support the strut that pinned George's shoulder, as the fire and rescue team lifted the seat, with George in it, out of the car.

In a triumph of good timing, which was consistent with the rest of the operation, a dull beat announced the sound of the arrival of the air ambulance, which would reduce George's travelling time into the main hospital in Cardiff from over an hour to minutes. Emma stretched her aching limbs, stumbling over to the Mini. She pulled an oversized T-shirt from the boot over her head, which was enough to shield her as she wriggled out of her bloodstained shirt and then opened a bottle of water, using it to wash her hands before walking over to Tess. The ambulance driver who was sitting with her got to his feet, saying he had some calls to make and leaving the two women alone.

Tess was cradling one hand in her lap, and Emma could see that, above the wrist support she'd been given, her fingers were swollen. She sat down next to her.

'He'll be all right, Tess. It all looks really scary, but that's because everyone's doing their best to keep the injury to George's shoulder stable. Josh is making a decision now about whether they can lift George out of the seat without doing any damage to his shoulder.'

'Thank you.' Tess shrugged tearfully. 'Will he be able to use his arm?'

'I don't know the full extent of his injury, Tess, none of us will until he's in surgery. What I can tell you is that Josh has done everything he can to minimise the damage, and that the surgeons will do all they can to restore the use of that arm. The techniques they use...' Emma shrugged, grinning at Tess. 'You don't really need chapter and verse about the techniques, do you? Just that some of them look a lot like miracles.'

'I've had my miracle for the day. You and Josh found us, and... I care about George's arm, of course, but all I really need him to do is to stay alive.'

Emma put her arm around Tess's shoulders wishing that she knew how it felt, to have someone whose name was the first thing on your lips when you were hurt and frightened. She'd seen it time and time again, in the course of her work, but she'd never worked with Josh before. Today had made her feel that calling *his* name might not be a completely outrageous thing for her to do.

Although he wouldn't hear... Josh would be staying in London after the rally, and she'd be going back to Liverpool. She might want him around in an emergency, but their differences were too great to withstand the everyday. That was the test that George and Tess had taken on, and they seemed to have passed with flying colours if their easy camaraderie over the last week was anything to go by.

Tess was hugging her tight, and right now nothing else mattered. The air ambulance flew over their heads, and Emma looked across at the team working with George. Josh must have decided it was safe to take him out of the car seat, and was supervising his transfer onto a carrycot from the ambulance.

The air ambulance was coming in to land now, and it looked as if they'd be on the move soon. Emma waited for the roar of the rotor blades to subside, so that they could talk again.

'Has the ambulance driver said where they'll be taking you, Tess? If he gives me directions I'll follow you.' It looked as if Josh would be going with George, and Emma hoped that Griff wouldn't get distressed when he saw Josh leave. He'd been sitting in the back of the Mini, quietly watching through the open window, and even when the helicopter had landed he hadn't started to bark. That was yet another miracle to add to the total for today.

'Don't you worry about that, Emma, you've done more than enough already. They're sending someone from the GDK Foundation to meet me at the hospital. I'll be fine.' Tess smiled up at the ambulance driver, who was walking back towards them. 'Has everything been sorted out, Henry?'

Henry squatted down in front of her. 'Yes, your husband's going straight to the main hospital in Cardiff. Apparently the man you were with is a surgeon, so he's going to accompany him in the air ambulance.'

'Josh?' Tess turned to Emma.

'Yes, that's right. Josh will take really good care of George and he'll be able to speak to the surgeon in Cardiff and tell him exactly what's happened. That'll help with the decisions he has to make about how best to repair the damage to George's shoulder.'

Henry nodded. 'And as for you, Tess, I've called your rally people back and they said that Erica from the GDK Foundation is at the local hospital waiting for you. You know her?'

Tess smiled at him. 'Yes, I know Erica. Thank you.'

'Right. I'll make sure that Erica has the number for the Cardiff hospital, where they're taking your husband, and as soon as we've finished with you at the local hospital, she'll take you there.'

'Thank you, Henry.'

It seemed that Emma would be making the journey to Cardiff on her own. Josh was needed elsewhere, and she'd have to make do with giving Griff a few extra-large hugs instead. Emma helped Tess to her feet, and she and Henry walked slowly with her to the back of the ambulance.

'I wish I was going with him.' Tess looked back at the air ambulance, tears in her eyes.

'I know. The best thing you can do for George

right now is to let Josh take care of him.' Emma put her arm around Tess's shoulders. 'I promise he will take really good care of him.'

'I know. Thank you. Will you… Can you tell him that I love him?' Tess seemed a little bashful in sharing the message with Emma, but it was obviously important to her.

'I'll go and speak to Josh now. I dare say you know what his answer's going to be.'

Tess blushed slightly. 'Yes, I know.'

Emma left Henry to settle Tess in the ambulance and jogged back towards the group who were clustered around George. Josh saw her coming and turned to her. There was time enough for a few words…

'Tess has a message for George. Tell him that she loves him.'

Josh smiled. 'I'll make sure to tell him.'

'Okay. I'll…um…see you later on? At the hotel?'

'I may be a while, but if you want to wait here, I'll head back and we'll finish the drive to Cardiff.'

'It doesn't matter how long you are. I'll wait.' Josh knew how much this meant to her. She'd wait all day and all night for him if he said he was coming back.

He shot her that melting blue-eyed look of his.

The one that said she could trust him. 'Sit tight, then. I'll see you later.'

Emma had called the rally supervisor, and he'd said that there would be someone there to check them in, whatever time they arrived. He would also arrange for the local car club, who were helping with this leg of the rally, to come out and salvage whatever was left of Tess and George's car.

It didn't seem that there was a great deal to salvage, but Emma had been around car enthusiasts all her life, and seen gleaming cars carefully reconstructed from husks that were much more damaged than this. If George and Tess wanted to spend the next phase of their retirement recreating the Alpha, then at least they'd have the chance to do so, and she guessed she wouldn't be alone in showing up and offering to help. Emma let Griff out of the Mini, fastening his lead to his collar, and took him on a long walk to find and retrieve the various car parts that were scattered along the Alpha's trajectory from the road to the tree trunk.

A taxi brought Josh back, almost three hours later, as she was finishing what was left of the sandwiches that had been stowed away in the boot of the Mini, out of Griff's reach. By yet another miracle, he was holding a paper carrier bag and two large cardboard cups.

'Coffee?'

He sat down beside her on the grass. 'No. What do you want with coffee, when I have a nutritionally balanced, high-roughage health drink for you.'

Emma grabbed one of the containers. 'It's coffee. I can smell it.'

'I've got sandwiches as well.' Josh snatched the carrier away, as Griff ambled over to investigate it.

'You can share them with Griff. I've just eaten all the emergency sandwiches I had in the boot.'

'You had emergency sandwiches?' Josh turned the corners of his mouth down. 'I wish you'd told *me*.'

'And when were you going to eat them? You were busy. How's George?'

'In surgery. It looks as if they'll be able to get the strut out without damaging the primary nerves, but we'll have to wait and see. I left before Tess arrived—I didn't want her to see me with George's blood all over my shirt—but I called her from the taxi and gave her an update.' He took a long swig of his coffee, throwing Griff's ball, and the dog ran after it barking joyfully.

He left the bag of sandwiches on the grass beside her and got to his feet, opening the boot of the Mini and pulling a clean shirt out of his bag. Then Josh glanced back in her direction.

'Turn around.'

He'd caught her staring and stopped unbuttoning his shirt.

'What do you mean turn around? You're happy to take your shirt off in full view of any passing motorists, but I have to turn around?'

'Yeah, you do.' Josh grinned suddenly. 'That's our deal.'

Shame. He was right though, they needed rules that they could stick to. Particularly now, when she felt so close to him. Emma turned around, picking up her coffee cup. 'Remind me, Josh. What did *you* do after you helped me out of the car this afternoon?'

'That was a friendly kiss. On the cheek.'

So it *was* a kiss. Emma heard his footsteps behind her and wiped the smile off her face before he sat down next to her, rolling the sleeves of his shirt up.

'I'm reckoning that honesty's a part of the deal too. You were so brave, and I couldn't help it.'

'Not reckless?' She'd been hoping that the word hadn't occurred to Josh.

He shook his head. 'You were able to squeeze in there a lot better than I could. And maybe you just went ahead and did it because you thought I'd object…'

'That crossed my mind. I thought you'd understand though; you had everything pretty well planned out.'

'Not...down to the last excruciating and needless detail?'

He remembered what Emma had said to him, just as clearly as she remembered what he'd said to her. 'No. None of the details were excruciating or needless.'

'Right. Glad we spoke, then.' Griff returned with the ball, dropping it at his feet, and Josh threw it again.

'I see you've organised for the Alpha to be salvaged.' He gestured towards the now empty piece of grass where George's car had come to rest. 'Should we go and check that nothing's been left behind?'

'No, the local car club came and did it. About twenty of them turned up, and they were really organised and got everything loaded up in the back of a truck in less than an hour. *And* they swept with metal detectors to make sure they hadn't missed anything. We can get back onto the road as soon as you've eaten and I've drunk my coffee.'

Josh nodded, obviously turning something over in his mind. Then he turned to her. 'It was nice working with you, Emma.'

That meant a great deal, and Emma needed to tell him. This was the first and last time they'd find themselves working together like this, and she wouldn't have the chance to say it again. They'd already left far too much unsaid.

'We did more than just working together, didn't we? You were the friend who gave me the strength to do what needed to be done. And you're the friend who came back for me, to finish today's leg of the rally.'

He smiled suddenly. 'This friendship thing. I'm starting to really like it.'

CHAPTER FIVE

JOSH WAS TIRED. Not just I-could-go-to-sleep tired, but the kind of tired he remembered from his first year of surgical training. The last few days had been non-stop, trying to fill in for David, take part in the rally and get his head around his relationship with Emma. Then the intense concentration involved in getting George out of the car and keeping his mind on the road as they drove into Cardiff, stopping to complete all of the challenges as they went.

'You're out of time for any bonus points on today's leg.' The steward who was waiting for them at the finishing point in Cardiff shook both his and Emma's hands. 'But congratulations, both of you.'

Emma had smiled up at him, and Josh had felt suddenly awake. The sensation didn't last long though, and by the time they'd parked and made their way across to the hotel, he was beginning to doze on his feet.

'I spy a coffee lounge.' Emma tugged at his sleeve. 'I wonder if they do cocoa?'

'I expect they do, but I'm going to have to take a rain check. I need to take Griff for a walk and then do the blog post for tonight.' Josh looked down at Griff, who wasn't displaying his usual excitement at hearing the word *walk*. Emma looked almost as tired as he felt, and perhaps Griff's team instinct was kicking in and he'd decided to curl up and fall asleep too.

'I took him for a walk *and* spent an hour throwing his ball for him—that's got to be enough for today surely. And how long is the blog post going to take, fifteen minutes? You could do it over cocoa...'

Emma seemed determined to divert him and it *was* tempting. Very tempting, particularly as the coffee lounge had deep armchairs to sink into and the thought of relaxing with her at the end of a long day when so much had happened seemed like perfect bliss at the moment.

'Fifteen minutes for you, maybe. It took me three hours and a call to GDK's head of IT to get it right last night. I'm not the founder of the organ recipients blog, remember?' That had just slipped out. Something from their past together; in fact, pretty much the first good thing from their past that either he or Emma had spoken about.

'Well, that's just outrageous. Three hours and

a phone call, and you couldn't even get the photographs lined up?' Emma had clearly been checking yesterday's blog out.

'Like I say.' Josh grinned down at her, the familiar forthright humour sending tingles down his spine. 'I don't have your natural ability.'

'Clearly not. Give me your laptop.' She held out her hand. 'We'll have some cocoa, you can show me where everything is and then you can go out with Griff if you think he wants a walk. I'll have it done by the time you get back.'

'You don't need…' Actually, he wanted her to. Very much.

'I'm not taking any arguments, Josh. We're in this together.'

It really felt as if they were. Josh gave in to the inevitable, opening his bag and handing his laptop over. They found a sofa where Emma could look over his shoulder at the screen, and Griff needed no encouragement to curl up in the space under the coffee table for a snooze. A waiter brought two cups of cocoa, and Josh opened his email, downloading all of the attachments and logging on to the GDK Foundation's blog.

'All right. I can take it from here.' She tugged at the corner of the laptop and Josh handed it over.

Emma set to work, cropping photographs and adding captions, seeming to know exactly how much to cut to make the images seem as vibrant and full of life as she was. She was absorbed in her task, but she turned suddenly as if a thought had occurred to her.

'You've decided against taking Griff for a walk?'

Josh nodded down towards Griff, whose paws were twitching, clearly in the grip of some doggy dream. 'I might have to carry him, and that rather defeats the object. I'm watching and learning.'

She grinned at him. 'Right, then. You want me to go a bit slower?'

Nope. The regular, repetitive actions on the screen, along with the quiet rattle of the beads around Emma's wrist, were strangely soothing. Josh stretched his legs out in front of him, leaning back on the soft cushions...

'Ow!'

Waking a guy up with a soft kiss... Josh knew full well that Emma knew how to do that. Clearly she also knew exactly how to wake someone up with an elbow to the ribs. He hoped that his reaction had satisfied all of her expectations.

She was smirking. Clearly it had.

He wiped his hand across his face, trying to gather his thoughts. 'Am I supposed to say *sorry* for falling asleep on you?'

Her smile broadened. 'Didn't I just relieve you of the necessity?'

'Probably. You've finished?' Josh leant over and saw that the screen displayed the new blog. 'It looks good. I really appreciate it.'

She nodded, brushing his thanks away. 'I might take the job over. Since I'm better at it than you.'

She did that a lot. Cloaked her kindness with a brisk smile and a smart answer. Josh was just wondering whether he ought to point that out, when a tone sounded from his laptop and a box popped up on the screen announcing a video call. He felt Emma jump, and move suddenly away from him, out of range of the camera, and realised their shoulders had been almost touching.

'What does David want?' Emma's tone held the implication she'd been caught doing something she shouldn't.

'I have no idea. I expect it's about what happened today.' Josh reached forward and answered his father's call.

'Dad. How are things?'

David smiled. 'Fine. Very good. I heard about George and Tess.'

'I guessed you must have. Erica called you?'

'Yes. What's your assessment, Josh?'

'I had a word with the surgeon who was going to operate on George's shoulder, and stayed while they took X-rays and did some tests. First indications are that the strut from the car hasn't caused major damage, and that in time and with some intensive physiotherapy he may well recover full use of his arm.'

David nodded. 'Good. And Tess?'

'Fractured wrist along with some cuts and bruises. Erica found a nice hotel close to the hospital and is staying with her tonight.'

'That's great. I've told Erica that I'll personally cover anything that they need, including physiotherapy and ongoing medical consultation for George.'

That was exactly as Josh would have expected. 'Thanks, Dad.'

'It made a lot of difference that you and Emma were there. I hear you both played a big part in getting George out of the car without making his injuries any worse.'

Suddenly, Josh wanted his father to know. That Emma was here, and that after all the pain and uncertainty of the past they'd finally managed to do something good together. Maybe Emma did too, because suddenly she leaned over, smiling into the camera.

'Hi, David. I'm right here, so don't say anything too nice about me.' She grinned brightly and David's fleeting look of surprise turned into a smile.

'Sorry, Emma. I think I'm going to have to embarrass you. You and Josh did a fine job. The fact that you then went on to finish the course and secure your sponsorships for the day is an added bonus.'

'I waited with the car and Josh came back for me.' The small catch in her voice told Josh that it had meant something to her. He'd hoped it had.

David nodded, taking a sip of his drink. Emma was staring fixedly at the screen now, as if something wasn't quite right. 'How are things going in Liverpool?'

'Well. Very well. In fact, I have some good news… Although I wanted to tell you in person, Josh.'

David always reckoned that good news was better in person, and Josh was inclined to agree with him. 'We'll be in London in a few days. You're coming down for the wrap party, aren't you?'

'I wouldn't miss it for the world. I'll catch you then and we can talk. How's Griff?'

'Asleep at the moment. Hold on…' Emma ducked down, rubbing behind Griff's ears to wake him, in a much gentler fashion than she had Josh. The sound of David's voice prompted a frenzy of tail-wagging, and when they said their goodbyes David was all smiles. It was good to see him so relaxed and happy.

'I wonder what the news is…' Josh closed his

laptop, glancing at Emma, who was pressing her lips together thoughtfully. 'You know, don't you?'

She jumped like a startled gazelle. 'No! Um... David should tell you.'

She knew. Josh leaned back on the sofa. 'Five days. It's a long time for you to hold out.'

Emma reddened.

'Especially when I'll be catching you unawares, asking you when you least expect it. Watching every move, putting two and two together...'

'Don't! Josh, it's their news, not mine.' She clapped her hand over her mouth, reddening even more.

'See. Two minutes and it's *their* news, not just Dad's.' Josh was brimming with curiosity now. 'You can't hold out, Em, you'll tell me sooner or later.'

Emma puffed out a breath. 'Stop looking at me like that, Josh.'

Josh was quite aware he'd been looking at her—who wouldn't look at Emma whenever they got the chance—but *like that*? Maybe his gaze still did have some effect on her, and if it was a fraction of the seductive warmth that hers had on him, she'd tell him everything. When he smiled, Emma rolled her eyes and puffed out a breath.

'Don't make things easy on me, will you? I suppose...it wouldn't do any harm to get used to the idea before David breaks the news. I'd like to put it on record that you forced this out of me though.'

'I applied intolerable pressure.' He could put a little more pressure on her and kiss her. Right now. Anytime, in fact. Sadly, it looked as if that wasn't going to be necessary.

'David was sitting on Val's sofa. And did you see that purple mug with the hedgehogs on it that he was drinking out of? That's Val's favourite mug. She never gives it to anyone else.'

Josh stared at her. 'Dad and Val?'

'It would explain where Val kept disappearing off to during the first week of the rally. *And* the dangly earrings.'

'Dangly earrings? Is that code for something?'

'No, but Val made them from the jar of beads we brought along. She never wears dangly earrings.'

Josh thought back. 'I remember them now. They suited her.'

'And your father clearly agreed.'

Josh thought for a moment. 'Do you think I should call him back?'

Emma looked at him pleadingly. 'And say what? That I just told you his big secret? He obviously wants to tell you face to face.'

'Yeah, I expect he does. I'd like it better too. You can't really shake someone's hand and slap them on the back via the internet. It's about time he turned his mind to something other than work.'

'It's about time Val let someone into her life too.' Emma was fiddling nervously with the beads at her wrist. 'It's really not weird at all, is it…?'

It might have been…slightly…if his and Emma's relationship had survived. 'Nah. Maybe we can just say that we played our part in bringing them together. Since we were both so understanding about their sneaking off in the evenings.'

Emma puffed out a relieved breath. 'Yes, that's nice. You don't mind?'

Josh shook his head. 'It's been twenty years since my mum died. Dad's been alone for a long time, and Val's perfect for him. We'll give them a bit of space and let them tell us in their own time.'

Emma puffed out a breath of relief. 'Thank you.'

'Now I know how Dad felt when I first brought a girl home.' Josh couldn't help smiling at the sudden reversal of roles.

'How's that?'

'Well… I really hope he doesn't do anything stupid and mess this up.'

'I was just thinking that about Val. I reckon they'll manage just fine without us.'

They were both laughing now, and Josh realised that his arm was around Emma's shoulders. He wasn't entirely sure how it had got there, just that it felt right. Josh had never realised just how good they could be together as friends, and he was still coming to terms with that.

Coming to terms with it didn't mean taking things any further. They'd tried that already and it hadn't worked so maybe Josh should be concentrating on not messing up with Emma. He let her go, and leant forward, picking up his laptop and hugging that instead.

'I really *have* to sleep.'

Emma nodded. 'Me too. I'll see you in the morning.'

The next morning Josh woke late, to find Griff sprawled across his chest and licking his cheek. He'd dreamed that it was Emma, only she'd been kissing him and her breath smelled sweet. Josh groaned, pushing Griff's nose out of his face, and stomped downstairs to enquire as to why the hotel staff hadn't given him his early morning wake-up call.

It turned out that Emma had cancelled it. The Mini was gone from the hotel car park and Josh combined Griff's morning walk with a jog over to where they'd be lined up for the awareness event. Cardiff was one of the three most important capital city stops and he couldn't help feeling annoyed. That evaporated slightly when he saw that the event was in full swing, and glimpsed Emma right in the thick of things, giving out leaflets and talking to people who were crowding around her car.

'All right, you made your point. You didn't need me, after all.' The thought hurt more than it should because Emma looked particularly radiant today, dressed in a blue miniskirt with a matching longline jacket, her hair caught up in curls and shining in the sun.

'Oh, Josh! Of course we need you. What about all the calls you've been making from the car to organise things, while you're trying to navigate?'

'*Trying* to navigate? We haven't missed anything, have we?' He was still feeling a little grumpy.

'No, we haven't, which only goes to show that you can do two things at once. All the work you've done to hold the rally together means that it isn't going to collapse in a heap if you get a bit of sleep.' Her attention was caught suddenly by a little boy who was tugging at her skirt. 'Hi, sweetie. Where's your mum and dad?'

The boy pointed over to a couple who were standing a few yards away and Emma nodded to them, then bent down to hear what he was saying. 'You want a car like this when you grow up? With sunshine around the wheels?'

She leaned forward, again nodding as the boy whispered something else. 'Is he? What's your brother's name?' The boy whispered again and Emma smiled. 'Well, thank you for coming here today to tell me about him.'

Emma beckoned the parents over and turned to Josh. 'Matthew's brother has just been put on the list for a kidney transplant. And he'd like to go for a ride in the Mini so... I think I've just found a new navigator. You're out of a job there too.'

The mischief in her smile when she said it made Josh laugh. 'Okay. Message received and understood.' He turned to Matthew's parents, holding out his hand. 'Hi. I'm Josh Kennedy. I'm a transplant surgeon and I'm here with the GDK Foundation today. I gather your son is waiting for a new kidney...?'

The last few days had been unbroken sunshine. They'd driven across the Severn Bridge, and into England, stopping in Bath. Emma had accompanied Josh and Griff on a long walk, which took in the outside of some of Bath's more famous tourist attractions which were all closed for the day.

'It would be nice to come back and sample the Roman baths, sometime.' She wasn't sure whether Josh's comment was just a comment or an invitation.

'Yes, it would.' Emma wasn't sure either whether her reply was an acceptance or not.

The next morning she woke to an almost night-time darkness in the sky. Heavy thunderclouds covered the sun, and she added a black plastic mac and sou'wester that she'd found in a vintage shop to her outfit. As they drove out of Bath the skies opened and it began to rain heavily.

'Had to happen, I suppose.' The windows in the Mini were misting up, already. One of the disadvantages of a classic car was that they were considerably more comfortable to drive in good weather.

'Yeah, we've been lucky with the weather so far.' Josh leaned forward, wiping the windscreen so that she could see out as thunder rolled in the sky over their heads.

They made it out of Bath, the route winding through minor roads until there was a short stretch on the busy road that passed Stonehenge. Of course there were pictures to be taken, and Emma found a spot where she could pull off safely.

'Here we go, then. Time to get our feet wet.' She reached for her mac and sou'wester that were rolled up under the seat. They had to take turns, Josh getting into his waterproof jacket first, while Emma squashed herself against the driver's door, and then giving Emma room to pull on her mac.

Stonehenge stood in the distance, surrounded by mist, the dark clouds blending with the grey stones. This seemed like the best way to see it, travellers arriving after a long journey as they had for thousands of years. Griff was more than happy to stay in the car, while Emma shivered and posed for a photograph, water trickling down her neck.

As Josh was wiping the lens on his phone camera, a flash rent the sky, followed by the deep growl of thunder. Then another...

'Josh! Did you get it?'

'Think so...' He turned, running for the cover of the car.

Griff protested a bit, shaking himself as scattered drops of water landed on him when they got back out of their coats. Then Josh handed her the phone, and Emma flipped through the pictures.

There were a couple of her standing in the rain, then one blur as he'd raised the phone quickly and then the perfect shot. Thunder and lightning over Stonehenge. Despite the busy road on one side of them, the one-angled view of the camera made it seem that she was standing alone, in a wild and mysterious landscape.

'Ah! I love it, Josh!' She stared at the photograph.

'Worth getting wet for?'

'Yes, absolutely. Don't you think it's wonder-ful?'

He laughed, nodding. Josh might be ever prac-tical, but he always appreciated a bit of outra-geous fun when it presented itself. 'Yeah. It's wonderful.'

They kept driving, back on the country roads now. They were easier because there wasn't so much traffic, but Josh had to keep a close watch for hazards. The skies cleared, and then closed over again, a sudden, heavy downpour bounc-ing water from the surface of the road. Emma stopped the car, peering ahead of them.

'What do you think?' A stream of water was crossing the road, moving fast down the hill. A tractor was negotiating its way slowly through it, but the Mini was a lighter, lower vehicle.

'We can't get through that, Em.' He noted the time and the hazard ahead of them on his navi-gation notes. 'Hold on, I'll ask this guy if there's a different way round.'

He donned his jacket again, running to the side of the tractor that had stopped right in front of them. Their conversation seemed to involve a fair bit of pointing and then Josh ran back to the car, raising his hand in thanks to the tractor driver as he started his vehicle and drove away. He took his jacket off before he got back into the car this time, letting it shield him from the worst of the downpour as Emma leaned over, pushing the door open.

'He says we'd have to go all the way back to where we turned onto this road, and around...' Josh traced his finger on the map, along the route they'd have to take. 'But this road always floods in heavy rain and it'll drain off down the hill pretty quickly. He reckons if we wait half an hour there'll be no problem getting through.'

'I say we wait, then. It'll take us more than half an hour to get round and we'll miss some of the clues for stops. We won't lose points for stopping as long as we note the hazard.'

'Yeah, agreed.' Josh put the map down, stretching his legs as far as he could. The windows of the car began to mist again, and Emma pulled off the road while she could still see well enough to manoeuvre. There was a long lay-by at the side of the road, suggesting cars regularly waited here in the rain.

'Where is everyone?' She scanned the empty road. Any delays usually precipitated a small tailback of rally cars, as the gaps between them closed up.

'Maybe they've stopped further back. I dare say they'll be catching up with us when this downpour eases.'

Josh looked around as Griff began to register

his disapproval of the situation. The back window was leaking, drips of water getting in through the rubber window seals, landing on his nose and ears. Emma stretched back, but couldn't reach the seat belt clip.

'Josh, let him come in the front with us.'

He reached back, and Griff scrambled forward, onto her lap. Emma hugged him and he quietened down a bit.

'You okay?'

There was no escaping Josh's perceptive gaze. Maybe she didn't want to.

'That seal's always leaked a bit. My dad did everything he could with it, but when it rained really heavily like this I still used to get wet in the back of the car. Mum kept a little waterproof jacket to cover me up with.' Those old memories seemed so much more precious now.

'If this is the only leak, your dad did a good job.'

Josh always remembered to acknowledge the things that Dad had done with the car over the years. Emma liked that he did, but the moment seemed even more bittersweet for it. She stroked Griff's ears, too wary of reaching out for Josh, which was what she really wanted to do.

'I miss him.'

Josh nodded. 'Yeah. It's only been a year.'

'I thought things were supposed to get better

after a year.' That's what all the articles she'd read said.

He reached over, his fingers stroking Griff's head. It seemed that Griff was getting all the human contact that Emma really wanted with Josh. 'I suppose if you want to draw up a time-table, then a year might be a ballpark figure to play with. You said you stayed with your mum for six months afterwards, before moving down to Liverpool?'

Emma nodded. 'Yeah, she needed me around for a while. Then she told me that she was fine and that she wanted me to go and live my own life.'

'Has it ever occurred to you that those six months were mainly taken up considering her needs? And that she made you go so that you could start feeling the things you needed to feel?' Josh's voice was tender.

'No, it hasn't. I guess Mum's a bit smarter than me.'

Josh shook his head. 'She's just seen a little more, that's all.'

'You still miss your mum, don't you?' Emma knew that Josh did, although he never spoke about it.

'Yeah. It does stop tearing at you though. Dad helped me a lot with that, even though he was grieving for her as well.'

That was a good way to describe it. Emma could operate perfectly normally, but there always seemed to be something tearing at her.

'I just feel…you know, that we always moved around a lot, for Dad's job. I loved it, a new place every summer when he went to join a different archaeological dig. When he was ill, he would tell me not to bother about him, and that I should be living my life. Keeping my wheels turning…' A tear rolled down Emma's cheek.

Josh leaned over, brushing it away. The contact meant everything, because it *was* so fleeting, and even though it was inevitable that they touch in this confined space, they'd always done so before by mistake.

'That's a hundred percent right and a hundred percent wrong, all at the same time, isn't it?' Josh was thoughtful.

'And how do you calculate the maths of that?'

'Something Dad said to me when my mum died.' He grinned suddenly. 'Imagine us carting bricks…'

'Difficult…' Emma closed her eyes and the picture in her head made her smile. 'I'm imagining.'

'He said he wasn't sticking with me out of duty, and there were times when it wasn't much of a pleasure. He was doing it because it was his *right*. It was your right to stick by your dad when he

was ill, and I'm guessing that both your parents understood that, and that you have no regrets about exercising it.'

'No, I don't. What's the other side of the equation?'

'That, right now, you can remember the part about living your life. Keeping your wheels turning.'

Emma opened her eyes. 'I came on the rally thinking that driving all this way would be a way of doing that. At the moment though it just seems that I'm on the move but still stuck in the same place.'

'Give it time. You'll find that feeling of moving forward again. You're at your best with your wheels turning.'

It was nice of him to say that, considering it was what had broken them up in the first place. A car drew up in the lay-by behind them, and they both looked round.

'That's Ryan and Kaitlin.' The celebrity duo seemed to have decided to wait in the car, which was wise because even though the downpour had eased off a bit it was still raining.

Josh nodded. 'I should go and have a word with them.' He hesitated, obviously wondering whether there was anything else that Emma wanted to say.

'Go. I'm going to do the really hard job and

keep Griff dry.' She grinned at him and Josh nodded.

'Okay. Well, good luck with that.' He reached for her again, brushing his fingers across the back of her hand. One tiny gesture, limited by all of the things that they were most afraid of, but it meant everything. And then he was out of the car, pulling his jacket around him as he jogged back to the other vehicle.

'How does that happen, eh, Griff?' Emma hugged him and he wriggled with joy, resting his head on her shoulder. 'That we're so alike and yet so different.'

Griff didn't know, and neither did Emma. Maybe Dad and Josh were both right, and if she just kept the appearance of moving forward, one day she really would.

CHAPTER SIX

JOSH HAD CALLED David from the car that morning, when it had become apparent that the Salisbury event was going to be washed out. His father had told him to leave it with him, and as they crossed the finishing line, and were directed over to a large standing area for the cars, it became apparent that David had anticipated the possibility of rain and his contingency plans had swung into action. Emma caught her breath.

'David called out the army?' There were a couple of squaddies in waterproofs, directing cars into a line, at the edge of a long awning that protected the information tables and people who'd come to watch from the rain.

'Do you know how many contacts Dad has?' Josh chuckled.

'Well…yes, but…' Emma waved brightly to the squaddie who was indicating the Mini's place in the line. 'Thank you!'

Josh found the senior officer present, and shook his hand, thanking him. Emma pressed a leaflet into his hand, her impish smile suggesting that since he was here he may as well take one, and the officer smiled, beckoning to one of his men and telling him to make himself useful and give some leaflets out. He then turned back to Josh, asking how his father was these days. Clearly the foundation had been of assistance to him at some point, and he'd welcomed the chance to volunteer for this.

The event was smaller than planned, but everyone being squashed together to keep out of the rain had injected a camaraderie into the proceedings. He took some photos, emailing them to David, who replied with a smile emoji. He and Emma got back to their hotel late, after having helped with the clearing up, and he left Emma at the door of her room, expressing a craving for a very long, very hot shower. Josh went to his room, trying not to envision that.

The following day was bright and clear again, one of those days after heavy rain when everything seemed greener, even in the town. The trip from Salisbury to Brighton was a relatively long one and everyone was tired. The knowledge that London was only two days away now had become the driving force behind the smiles and camaraderie of the rally teams. When they crossed the county boundary from Wiltshire into Hampshire, Emma peeled out of the car, racing to pose for the camera next to the sign by the road. And Hampshire to Sussex elicited a whoop of joy that woke Griff up as he dozed in the back seat.

'Catch a falling star…' Emma frowned at the final clue that would gain them extra points. 'It'll be dark by the time we get to Brighton, so I suppose… Look for stars? Maybe there are some on the Brighton Pavilion; I've never noticed them.'

'We'll wait and see.' This was the one clue that Josh knew the answer to ahead of time. David had let it slip when he'd been talking about the arrangements for the rally.

'You *know*, don't you? Are you playing hard to get?'

'Yep. But I can't tell you. Dad swore me to secrecy.'

Emma frowned. 'So…how did you manage the fact that David knew the answers to all the clues? Were you two cheating?'

'No. He didn't tell me any of the others. When we were driving I had to get all of the clues for extra points.'

'Hmm. Very honourable of you both. And it's too late for me to try and wrestle the answer from you.' Emma shot him a mischievous look that, yet again, made Josh's insides go to jelly.

Just outside Brighton, the stewards stopped them, closing up the gaps between the cars so that they could drive through the town almost in procession. It was getting dark, and Emma was tapping her finger excitedly on the steering wheel and craning to look up for any stars that might be shooting across the heavens.

'It can't be *real* falling stars. It's a bit cloudy and David would have thought of that. He thinks of everything.'

'Yep.'

She turned to him. 'You mean, *Yes, it's real falling stars* or *Yes, David thinks of everything*?'

'Yep,' Josh teased her, and Emma puffed out an exasperated breath.

'Josh, so help me, I'm going to threaten you with something you won't like…'

There was nothing that Emma could do to him that he wouldn't like. Josh let the idea simmer in his mind for a moment, and the car jolted as she put her foot on the accelerator to move forward another hundred yards.

When they reached the town centre the streets were alive with people, just as you'd expect from an early summer's Friday evening in Brighton. Many had stopped to see the procession of cars, working its way down to the promenade, and the GDK Foundation's local supporters were out in force, giving out flyers along with card signs that were being waved enthusiastically.

Emma sounded the horn, in response to the

cheering and waving, and a few other cars followed suit. Josh reached back to lay his hand on Griff's head, but he was clearly loving the commotion going on around him.

'Is he all right?'

'He's fine. You know how Griff loves a crowd.'

'But where are the stars…?'

They inched down the hill towards the sea-front, and as the first cars began to turn left, three beams of light shot up into the air from somewhere out at sea, dipping and wheeling together. And then lasers from the buildings around them showered the street with light, falling stars playing around the rooftops.

'Ooh! Look, Josh!' Emma was practically dancing in her seat, pointing ahead of them. 'Look at the pier!'

The small boats that David had arranged were invisible in the gathering gloom, as were the careful calculations that were behind the laser show. The magic of stars, falling from the top of the Palm Court, and drifting down into the sea was all that Emma saw, and it was suddenly all that mattered.

'You like it?' Silly question. It was clear that Emma *loved* this.

'No. It's horrible. I want to go home.' She turned to glance at Griff, who was standing on the back seat, wagging his tail furiously. 'Griff hates it as well.'

'Okay. We'll go home, then.'

At the bottom of the hill, stewards were directing cars into the lane to turn left. Emma stopped the car and wound the window down.

'I want to go right.'

'No, love. If you go half a mile to the left, there's a section of the seafront that's been closed off…'

'Okay, I'll go left in a minute. I want to go right first.'

The steward frowned, and Josh leaned over. 'We'll go right first and then left.' He flashed the ID card clipped to the back of today's information pack that gave his name and bore the word *Organiser* in red at the top. The steward stepped back and waved them left.

'I didn't know you had that.' Emma grinned at him.

Josh shrugged. 'I haven't had to use it before now. Why are we going right?'

'The clue says *catch* a falling star. There's a place just a bit further down this way…'

'Right. I guessed it was something important.' Clearly most of the competitors were happy with just getting a photograph of the falling stars, but Emma had set her heart on catching one.

She drove a little way along the promenade,

and then turned right into a narrow side street, driving around the block to put the sea ahead of them again before she parked.

'What do you think?' Her hand grazed his sleeve and Josh shivered. Then she leaned towards him, as if trying to see exactly what he saw.

'Perfect.' It *was* perfect. A clear view of the pier smothered in stars. If they crossed the road and took the steps down onto the deserted beach, then Emma could reach up and the flattened perspective of the camera lens would see her catching stars. If that was what Emma wanted, then it was what *he* wanted too. Just to share in a little bit of her magic, before the opportunity was lost.

She was looking up at him, her eyes wide in the darkness. The street was deserted and the constant activity of the rally seemed a very long way away.

He reached for her and she didn't move back. In the warm welcome of her gaze, he summoned the courage to touch her, brushing his fingertips against the back of her hand. She curled her fingers around his, raising them to her lips.

Too much, and yet not nearly enough. It was what Emma had always been to him. She overwhelmed his senses, and he'd always wanted more, but was afraid to take it. But the possibility of catching stars meant that tonight was no time for fear.

'Em…?'

She lay one finger across his lips. 'I don't want you to think about it, Josh. You'll never do it if you do.'

Maybe she was right. He *couldn't* think at the moment. Josh folded his arms around her, and kissed her, feeling the warm sweetness of her lips…

A click sounded from the back seat, as the seat belt released. Griff was clearly feeling a bit left out, and he'd clambered forward and was doing his best to lick the side of Emma's face.

'Ew! Stop slobbering.'

'You mean Griff, I trust?' Josh caught Griff's collar, pulling him back. 'I haven't had much practice lately but…'

'Of course I mean Griff.' The light was still dancing in Emma's eyes. 'And *out of practice* really suits you.'

Good to know. He'd felt her hunger too, and Josh couldn't let this go. He wound his free hand around her waist, and Emma wrapped her arms around his neck, pulling him towards her. She kissed him with all the sweetness and magic that he remembered her for, the feeling even more intoxicating for having missed this so much.

It was even more amazing for being so awkward—trying to hold Griff back, while also finding a way to hold her in the tight space. He was a prey to Emma's hands, caressing his neck and sliding down to his chest. He shivered. There was no holding back, just a desperate craving for her.

She drew back just in time, before he lost all control.

'Hmm. Shooting stars.' Her eyes were still clouded with desire.

Shooting stars, streaking across the sky and then exploding, igniting an inferno. One that could so easily lead them into places that they really shouldn't go. Josh smiled at her.

'You want to go and catch one?'

She hesitated, her fleeting mask of disappointment matching his own feelings. 'Yes, I guess so. Even if ours were better.'

It was good to get out of the car, and into the cool evening air. When Josh examined the seatbelt clip, he could find no reason for its sudden failure, until Griff stood up on the seat, pulling the webbing tight and nonchalantly hitting the release with his paw. The restraint flew free and he heard Emma's snort of laughter behind him.

'Smart pooch. You've got to admit he has timing.'

Emma had the same capacity to laugh whenever things went wrong that his mother had had, and at the moment that thought didn't carry with it all the usual reservations. He grinned, clipping Griff's lead to his collar. Hopefully he hadn't found a way to get out of that yet, or they'd be spending the evening chasing after him on the beach.

She linked her arm in his as they crossed the road, walking down the steps to the sand. It took a while to find the exact place for the photograph, but that didn't matter, because the wind blowing in from the sea seemed to be bringing a new start with it.

After a few tries, Josh adjusted his camera phone to capture both Emma and the stars projected onto the pier. Some photos of Emma jumping and flailing wildly, and then doubled over with laughter and then everything came together, and he got the perfect shot. Emma, in mid-air, her fingers appearing to be almost in reach of the stars.

Then it was Griff's turn. She grabbed the extending lead from Josh, making a throwing movement with her arm. Griff took the bait and jumped for the invisible treat, and Josh managed to catch him, his nose extended up towards the stars. Unaware of this triumph, Griff started to nose miserably on the sand for his lost treasure and Emma turned her mouth down.

'What have I done? Poor Griff!'

Josh chuckled, spinning a treat from his pocket

in Griff's direction, which he caught adroitly. Emma ran towards him, straight into his arms.

'Josh to the rescue...' Suddenly she was still, staring up into his eyes. 'I missed you so much.'

'I missed you too.' He felt a lump form in his throat at the thought of the tearing longing that had never properly subsided. Wondering how she was, and what she was doing the whole time they had been apart.

'I...' She seemed to think better of what she was about to say, pressing her lips together.

Thinking twice didn't much suit her. 'You what?'

'I spoke to David. Asked after you...'

Maybe she was thinking that he'd like the idea that she hadn't just forgotten about him. He did, but...

'Dad never said.'

'No.' Emma laid her hands on his chest. 'I asked him not to.'

That was Dad all over. His honourable streak wouldn't allow him to betray a confidence, however much it cost.

'That's how he knew your father had died?' Josh had always wondered, but had pushed the question out of his mind, glad that he had the opportunity to at least write some words of condolence to Emma and her mother.

'Yes. He'd agreed to keep quiet about our conversations, but he told me he wouldn't keep that from you. I was glad he didn't, your note meant such a lot to both Mum and me.'

'You spoke with him more than once?'

She was suddenly still, all the excitement draining out of her. The tinderbox that had ignited passion between them also had the capacity to ignite all the feelings of anger that had burned in their hearts. Maybe that was inevitable. Josh couldn't hold her any longer, and he turned away, walking towards the steps that led back up from the beach.

'What, Josh?' Emma couldn't let it go any more than he could, and she was following him, tugging at his arm. Rage floated over him, like a mist from the sea, seeping into his bones.

'So you were talking to my father, on a regular basis. But you didn't let him tell me how you were?'

'It's not his fault, Josh!' She frowned at him and, for once, Emma didn't seem to be able to divine what he was thinking. 'You know David...'

'I blame *you*, not him.'

Blame was an ugly word. But all the promise of their kiss, and then this sudden realisation... That was ugly too.

'I didn't want you to think that I was coming back, Josh. I wasn't.'

'But you still phoned Dad?'

the parked rally cars. It was a lot to expect of herself, but Emma did it anyway.

Anger was one of those convenient emotions that blocked everything else out. As hers started to fade, others started to crowd in. Hurt, that he couldn't see her point of view. Guilt, that she hadn't seen his. Confusion and despair. She'd had to call David about one of her patients, and asking about Josh had been an impulse that she'd regretted. One of those reckless things that Josh had accused her of. So she'd made David promise that he wouldn't tell Josh that she'd been asking after him.

And David, being David, had kept the promise. He'd called her back, to see how her patient was doing, and asked her to keep him updated. When her father had died, David had called her again, having heard from the hospital that Emma had taken a leave of absence.

None of that mattered, now. Maybe it was fate that they'd kissed and then argued. A reminder that they couldn't do all the same things a second time and expect the end result to be any different.

Josh must know that too, and when she managed to escape the festivities on the promenade, and drove back to her hotel for the night, he wasn't waiting for her. He was at a different, dog-friendly hotel tonight and that was probably for the best.

She borrowed a laptop from one of the other competitors, accessing her email online. Nothing from Josh—she didn't expect that—but the emails with the day's photographs had been automatically forwarded on to her account. The rally must go on, and she accessed the blog to post the photographs. She couldn't imagine how she and Josh would be able to get themselves to London tomorrow without a lot of shouting, but tomorrow was going to have to take care of itself.

too. Whatever he threw at her, she wouldn't cry, and she wouldn't hit back at him.

'Okay...?'

'I want to apologise. For the things I said and the way I said them.'

Emma shrugged miserably. 'It doesn't matter.'

'I called Dad last night.' He must have seen her alarm, because he shook his head. 'I didn't tell him anything about what happened, that's between you and me. I knew I'd been unfair, and wanted to know exactly what I need to apologise for.'

'You don't have to apologise for anything.' Although it meant something that he had.

'Dad told me that he'd been calling you as well, and that he'd asked you to keep him updated about your patient. And I do have something to apologise for, because I didn't listen when you tried to explain.'

Joy was beginning to seep through her. Right to her fingertips, which were tingling with the possibility that today might bring some kind of reconciliation. Emma walked over to him, sitting down next to Josh on the wall.

'I wasn't really *trying* to explain. I was too angry.'

'Yeah. I wasn't really trying to listen. I was too angry.'

CHAPTER SEVEN

JOSH MUST HAVE been up very early. Emma hadn't been able to sleep much, but when she went to check on the Mini the next morning he was already there, sitting on the low wall that surrounded the hotel car park, with Griff leaning against his legs. Even now, seeing him still made a lump rise into her throat.

Griff made a lunge for her, yelping excitedly and trailing the extending lead out to greet her. Emma bent down, wondering whether speaking only to Griff, the way they had at first, might work for them today as well.

'Hi...'

His one word was clearly for her and not Griff. Josh had obviously come to the same conclusion that she had and decided to put his own feelings on hold in favour of finishing the rally.

Emma swallowed hard. 'Hi. All set for today?'

He shook his head. 'Not even remotely. There's something I have to do first.'

He seemed calm and she should stay that way

Emma puffed out a sigh. 'We hurt each other, didn't we?'

Josh shook his head slowly, as if trying to make sense of it all. 'I was busy pretending to be one kind of person, but…when I was a kid I only had my mum. I used to make lists of people who might be there for me if something happened to her and…generally they were quite short.'

Josh and his lists. His flow charts. Emma was seeing all that in a different light, now.

'And I was on your list, and then disappeared. I'm sorry for that.'

He smiled suddenly. 'Sorry in an it's-all-my-fault kind of way? Or sorry that things happened the way they did?'

'The all-my-fault kind of sorry is tempting.' She smiled back at him. 'But since you mention it, I guess that I'm just sorry it happened and that you were so hurt by it. We should have talked more.'

Josh nodded. 'We're talking now…'

'Yes.' That felt good. As if there was some way to heal the past, even if they couldn't change it.

'You did the blog post.'

It was nice that he'd noticed. 'Of course I did the blog post. What, you were thinking that I'd be that petty?'

'Never. And it looks great, but I didn't send

you the best photographs. I emailed them this morning.'

Emma hadn't looked at her email yet. She pulled her phone out of her pocket and saw that she had mail from Josh, with two photographs attached. Her and Griff, reaching for stars.

'Have you had breakfast?'

Josh shrugged. 'Coffee.'

Now that she could bear to look him in the eye, Josh was clearly as tired as she felt. More coffee and a good breakfast would set them both up for the day.

'They've an outside dining area where we can sit with Griff, and if you bring your laptop I'll add the photos now.'

He reached down, opening the holdall at his feet. 'I've got something else for you.' Josh drew out his MP3 player and speaker.

'Mixtape?' Josh knew she liked a good music mix, and his were generally really good.

'Mixtape. I downloaded some sixties stuff last night.'

She could kiss him. Though maybe they weren't ready for that just yet, even if it would have been just a friendly kiss on the cheek.

'Thank you, Josh.'

He grinned broadly. 'My pleasure.'

Emma had outdone herself for this final leg of the rally. A suede miniskirt, with a matching fringed shoulder bag, and a bright swirly patterned blouse. Her hair was tucked up into a baker boy cap, and a pair of low-heeled boots finished off the outfit. Josh was beginning to really like sixties fashions.

She'd spent some time with a screwdriver, removing the seat-belt clip in the back of the car so they could secure the dual clip of Griff's harness to the housing behind the seat. Josh strapped him in securely, and Griff curled up on his blanket. The GDK volunteers were out again in force this morning, leafleting and waving to each car as it passed, and their progress through Brighton was slow. But soon enough they were on the open road, the sun rolling lazily across the chalk hills of the Sussex Downs.

'Oh… Turn that up, I love this one.' Emma's finger had been tapping on the steering wheel, in time with the mixtape.

'"Love in Pink"?' Josh grinned. 'You know that's my gran, don't you?'

'What? Cerise Kennedy is your grandmother? And you didn't tell me?' Emma took one hand off the steering wheel to give Josh a reproachful nudge. 'That's it, Josh Kennedy, I'm never speaking to you again.'

They'd been so bound up in each other during their short affair that nothing else seemed to exist. Josh could rectify that now.

'Shame. I won't be able to introduce her to you at the wrap party for the rally, if you're not speaking to me...'

'She's going to be at the wrap party? Cerise Kennedy?'

'Yep. Dad mentioned she'd be there last night. You are coming, aren't you?'

'Well, I am *now*.'

Clearly Emma had been reckoning on giving it a miss. Much as Josh had, last night. But now there was no question that they'd both be there. Emma was singing along with the chorus, and Gran would have appreciated her enthusiasm and the fact that she knew all the words, even if her hit and miss approach to the tune left something to be desired.

'Cerise Kennedy is David's mother. I can't believe it.'

'The clue's in the name.'

Emma shot him a pained look. 'Yes, but... She's so fabulous. And David's so sensible. Don't they argue?'

'They did have a falling out, some years ago. Gran was a single mum, and she never told Dad who his father was. He only found out when his father died and left him a fortune.'

Emma winced. 'Tricky...'

'Yeah, very. They weren't speaking for a couple of years. Even now, things aren't quite the same between them. They talk but they don't ever really say anything.'

'But if she's coming to the party…?'

'It surprised me when Dad said he'd invited her. I'm wondering if Val's influence has had some part in this, and keeping my fingers crossed that it's a sign that Dad and Gran have finally dug up the hatchet and burned it. Although, knowing Gran, there would have been a bit of drama involved along the way. They never let their differences affect me though. Even when he wasn't speaking to her, Dad still let Gran take me off on holidays and for weekends.'

'Because it was important for you to know that she was still there. You'd lost enough of your family already.' Emma was suddenly thoughtful.

'Yeah. Gran never let me go. She could have just disappeared from my life, or Dad could have shut her out of it, but they didn't. About the only thing they agreed on was that I needed to know they were both there for me, whatever their differences. She used to send me postcards from all the places she went on tour. I had hundreds of them.' Each one sent with love and adorned with Gran's ostentatious kisses at the bottom.

'She sounds wonderful. And I'm going to meet her…or at least maybe see her across the room…? Will she be singing?'

'You'll be meeting her. And Gran will definitely be singing, just try and stop her.'

'Fantastic. Go back…go back.'

Josh picked up the MP3 player, flipping the back button until 'Love in Pink' started to play again and Emma began to sing along, playing havoc with the tune all over again.

Maybe he should take a moment to revisit the idea that the complications of the situation between David and Cerise took any of the joy out of their reconciliation. Josh wasn't sure that he'd ever be entirely comfortable with Emma's wait-and-see attitude to the future, but maybe he could learn to live with it. Love it, even, the way he loved the optimism that went with it.

He glanced down at the map that had been lying forgotten on his knees. 'Wait… Stop!'

Emma came to an abrupt halt on the empty road. 'What?'

'That left turn we passed about half a mile ago. That's where we should be going.'

Still humming 'Love in Pink,' Emma turned the car in the road, heading back the way they'd come.

All of David's work, negotiating red tape and writing letters, had borne fruit. The cars travelled across Tower Bridge on a bright summer's day and snaked through London towards The

Mall, parking up on the borders of St James's Park, where preparations were already taking place for the Awareness Day tomorrow. When they'd crossed the last finishing line of the rally, Emma had let out a whoop of triumph, and Josh had added a round of applause. Even Griff had woken up from his sulk at no longer being able to free himself from his car harness and started to bark joyously. Josh knew that this was a personal triumph for her, and that she was sharing it with her father.

Emma got out of the car, chatting excitedly with the other drivers and the GDK Foundation volunteers, some of whom Josh recognised from Brighton, and who must have caught the train up to London so they could be there for both the start and the finish of today's run.

This was the end. The end of squeezing himself into a confined space. The end of laughing at Emma's terrible jokes and listening to her tone-deaf renditions of whatever song was playing in the car. The end of having to stop himself from taking her in his arms and kissing her.

It was for the best, because even if this was an ending, it might not be final. They'd both found some closure on the bitterness of their first parting, and this one carried with it some hope that in the future they might be able to greet each other as friends, rather than avoiding every mention of the other's name. It was time for him to take what he had, and leave.

But he didn't get away so easily. He felt a tug on his arm and turned around to find Emma there, holding two plastic cups.

'I got you some champagne. Just a taste, to celebrate.' She pushed one of the cups into his hand, tipping hers against it. 'We made it.'

'Yes, we did. Cheers, Em.' It sent a shiver of gratification through him that she wanted to share this toast with him. That she'd run after him, to do it.

'You're not going, are you?' She took a sip from her cup, looking up at him.

'I've got a long list of things to do for the wrap party that Dad emailed through, so I need to pop into the office.' That was largely true. He did have a long list, but it generally consisted of checking that everything had being done, and it would probably take Josh about half an hour to do that.

Emma turned the corners of her mouth down. 'But you'll be here tomorrow, won't you?'

'Yes, I'll be here. And there's still the party on Monday.'

That made her smile. 'Yes, I'm looking forward to that. I'll see you tomorrow, then.'

Walking away from her was hard. But Josh was going to have to get used to that.

CHAPTER EIGHT

THE LONDON AWARENESS event had been a massive success, and he and Emma hadn't had a chance to exchange more than a few words, there were so many people there. He'd caught her just as the day was winding down, asking what she'd be doing tomorrow, and Emma had blurted out something about dresses, highly secret missions and looking forward to seeing him at the party in the evening.

That was enough for Josh. The look on her face told him that he could anticipate a spectacular evening, and if it took all day to prepare for it, then that was good too. David would be driving down to London this evening, and Josh had said he'd call in on him first thing in the morning.

The next day went as planned. It was a pleasure to see David so happy and they'd talked all morning and gone for a long lunch together. Josh had popped into the hospital afterwards, finding that everyone was managing perfectly well without him, and then gone home to dress for the evening, a feeling of anticipation already livening his pace.

The GDK Foundation's office was a tall, white painted Georgian town house, in a quiet Notting Hill square. The steps up to the front door were flanked with torches, to add a little drama when darkness fell, and inside the reception area and the conference room had been cleared, and the partition between them folded back, to make one enormous space.

David always kept it simple for parties. The high ceiling, decorated with moulded plaster-work, and the shining parquet floor was enough to add grandeur. And Gran was more than enough to add sparkle.

Gran was obviously keeping an eye on each new guest as they entered, and she made a bee-line for him. Pink, sequins and fabulous were Cerise Kennedy's trademark, and tonight she'd outdone herself.

'Gran.' Josh bent to receive an air kiss. 'You look particularly wonderful tonight.'

'Thank you, darling. Let me look at you.' Gran stood back, smoothing her fingers across the lapel of his evening jacket. She gave a nod of approval, and then took his arm, leading him slowly across to the drinks table.

'I want a word with you, darling.'

Josh chuckled. Gran's cut-glass English accent had slipped momentarily into the Southern American drawl of her childhood. That usually happened when Gran expressed tenderness towards her family, and he suspected that he was in for one of her 'talks.'

Gran signalled to the waiter, who immediately poured two glasses of champagne, handing them both to Josh. Clearly Gran had everything under control already.

Which was no particular surprise. Gran liked to pretend that she hit the right note every time by serendipity, and that everything around her simply fell into place of its own accord, but she had a ferocious work ethic, and Josh knew that nothing around her happened by chance.

The light pressure of her fingers on his arm steered him over to the piano, which stood in one corner. There was a high stool next to it, under an arch of pink and silver balloons, which no doubt Gran had insisted on. She sat down on the piano stool, making room for Josh to sit with her, and accepting her glass from him with a little nod of thanks.

'Now, Josh. This whirlwind romance of your father's. You knew about it?'

'He didn't say anything, but Emma and I had worked out there was something going on. I didn't know he and Val were getting married until he told me this morning.'

'Emma?' Gran was always on the lookout for any romantic interest in Josh's life and she fixed him with a tell-me-more look.

'Emma was my driving partner for the second week of the rally after Dad and Val left for Liverpool. She's a good friend of Val's.'

'Oh.' Gran looked suitably disappointed, but rallied quickly. 'Well, this is very important. I'm sure that Val is perfectly nice, and your father seems blissfully happy, but I don't want you to think that she can ever replace your mother. Your father really loved Georgie…' Gran took his hand, squeezing it hard to emphasise the point.

'And it's obvious that he's head over heels in love with Val as well, Gran. I couldn't be more pleased for them both.'

'Ah!' Gran fanned her face with her gloved hand, as if she'd just averted a crisis. 'Well, I'm glad you feel that way, Josh. David will always be your father.'

'I know. Thanks, Gran.' Josh tipped his glass towards hers. 'We'll drink a little toast to them, shall we?'

'Indeed.' Gran was all smiles, now. 'I haven't met her yet. You'll have to point her out to me when she arrives…'

No need for that. There was a commotion in the doorway, and David and Val entered arm in arm. Josh hardly recognised Val. Her hair was swept sideways, curls cascading down one side of her face. She wore a dark green dress, the shimmering pattern of the black beads that covered it marking it as distinctly nineteen-twenties in style. At the hem, a glittering fringe of beads sparkled as she walked.

'Josh!' Gran grabbed his hand. 'Is that her?'

Josh wasn't sure how David could have made it any more obvious. He was looking down at Val with an expression on his face that was akin to worship. 'Yes, that's her.'

'She looks wonderful. And look at your father… Doesn't he look happy.' Gran let go of his hand, fanning her face again.

All those wasted years. His father and grandmother had both borne them stoically, but it was clear that they'd both been hurting. Maybe you never quite got over losing someone that you loved, and he would always miss Emma.

Josh leaned over towards his grandmother. 'Are we going over to say hello?' Gran always preferred to meet new people with someone on her arm to make the introductions.

'Thank you, dear.' Gran was dabbing at her nose with a filmy handkerchief that must have been in a concealed pocket in her dress. She may be glamorous, but she was also intensely practical. Josh stood, offering his arm to his grandmother.

Val looked a little nervous, but just as Gran was able to make people shake in their shoes with just one look, she also had the ability to make them feel at ease, and she'd clearly chosen the latter approach. She kissed David and then turned to Val, complimenting her on her dress and talking excitedly. David was beaming from ear to ear, clearly happy to have the chance to share this with Gran, and Val was smiling now too. Josh melted away quietly to watch.

'That's nice. Val was *terrified*.'

Josh turned to see Emma standing next to him. His heart began to thump.

Her hair was in a shining pleat at the back of her head, and she wore a high-necked halter dress, the pale blue fabric falling just above her knees and encrusted with swirls of beads and sequins. A nod to the sixties that was squeezing at his heart remorselessly.

'Emma.' It was the one and only word that summed up how gorgeous she looked.

'What? Are you all right?'

'No, I'm a long way from all right. Were you planning on having to resuscitate me when you dressed for the evening?'

Emma laughed. 'You scrub up pretty well yourself. And don't make me resuscitate you. I had to get Val to do deep breathing in the taxi on the way back from our shopping trip.'

'So *that* was what you were up to today?'

'Yes. Val wanted something that might allow her to subtly fade into the background.'

'She did? I'm afraid your secret mission failed, then.'

'I took her to a vintage clothes shop on the Kings Road and made her try on a few things. I think we've both blown a bit of a hole in next month's pay cheques, but you can't get away with incognito when you've got a rock like that on your finger. Have you seen it?'

'Not yet. Dad did Val proud?'

'Oh, yes. Diamonds and a beautiful green-blue aquamarine. Aquamarine's her birthstone and it matches her eyes.' Emma tucked her hand into his arm, murmuring quietly, 'Are you okay with this whirlwind proposal?'

'I'm really happy for them both. Care for some champagne, to celebrate?'

'Just water for me, please. I want to be stone-cold sober when I meet your grandmother so that I'm not tongue-tied with adoration.'

'I wouldn't worry too much on that score. Gran loves tongue-tied with adoration.'

Emma was officially bowled over. Josh's grandmother had insisted that she call her Cerise and whispered to her that she would be singing 'Love in Pink' especially for her. Josh had laughingly reminded her that Cerise might have promised just the same to a few other people, when they danced together to the song, but that didn't matter. Emma was happy to share.

The night was full of laughter and music. As people started to leave, she wanted to bar the doors and keep them here, in this bubble. Tonight should last, because tomorrow she'd be going back to Liverpool.

To her friends, her job, the small cottage in the suburbs that was her home for the time being. Keeping her wheels turning. But the only thing that seemed to mean anything at all was that she'd be leaving Josh behind in London.

Josh had sent David off home, taking the keys to the office from him so that he could lock up. Perfect timing, as always, because Val's bright excitement had begun to give way to fatigue.

'We're leaving… Going now…' David had smilingly called out the words, as he and Val twirled in a half-embrace, half-dance right to the front door. Then he escorted her down the steep steps, and into the nineteen-thirties Daimler that David had driven during the first week of the rally, which was waiting for them outside.

David was so good for Val. Somewhere out there, a guy who would be that good for Emma was waiting. Or maybe he was standing right next to her…

Liverpool. Tomorrow. Since the evening really *was* ending now, and people were leaving, everything she did had to be in that context.

'Darling…' Cerise looked as fresh as she had when Emma had first laid eyes on her, taking her hands between hers and dispensing air kisses. 'It was enchanting to meet you. The next time I'm in Liverpool, I'll have to show you a few of the places that have special memories for me.'

Cerise leaned in, whispering in her ear, and Emma's hand flew to her mouth.

'You didn't…'

'He wasn't a household name then. Very talented young musician though, and *very* handsome.' Cerise put her gloved finger to her lips and Emma smiled. Josh's gran had suddenly taken yet another step up in her estimation.

'Care to share that with me?' Josh gave Cerise hug goodbye.

'Of course not. It's a grandmother's prerogative to hint at youthful indiscretions without going into the details.'

'That's true. Particularly when the details might take a while.'

That was obviously Cerise's intended meaning, and she smiled, planting a kiss on Josh's cheek. He rubbed at the lipstick mark, and Cerise took the arm of the chauffeur who was waiting to escort her to her car.

Cerise had avoided smudging her lipstick all evening, but she was clearly willing to make an exception for her grandson. The way that Josh was grinning at her, as she turned for one final wave, told Emma that he was well aware of the privilege.

He walked next to her, back into the building, sorting through a bunch of keys as he went. 'Dad said that there was something you wanted to find from the library. You want the key?'

'Yes. Thanks.' They were getting closer and closer to their goodbye and Emma didn't really want to waste any of the precious time they had left together, but the GDK Foundation's library had material that was difficult to get elsewhere.

'I'll leave you to it, then.' Josh snapped the key from the ring and put it into her hand. 'I'll say goodbye to the last of the guests and take a walk round to check that no one's been locked in the bathroom.'

The caterers were busy clearing up, and they too would be gone soon. Emma walked through the glass-ceilinged conservatory at the back of the house, and opened the door at the far end, which led to the library. She found the paper she needed and switched on the scanner to take a copy.

Josh appeared in the doorway, just as she was finishing. 'All done?'

'One minute...' She found the space on the

shelf that she'd taken the publication from and replaced it. If she fussed over turning the scanner off for a moment, then maybe he'd turn away and stop looking at her like that. This parting was difficult enough already.

But he didn't. Emma switched off the light, and locked the library door, and he was still there. She dropped the key back into his hand and went to walk past him to get her coat, but the brush of his fingertips on her arm stopped her in her tracks.

They'd acknowledged a lot in the last week, and maybe saying this wasn't such a bad thing.

'It's been a wonderful evening, Josh. I didn't want it to end.'

'Does it have to?'

'Sometime. Unless you happen to have a time machine.' Not just for tonight. It would have to go back and change their whole lives, who they both were. All the things that were set in stone, now.

'Sometime isn't quite yet though.'

'It's soon. I have to go back up to Liverpool tomorrow afternoon.' And Josh would have to cross her off his list of people who wouldn't leave him behind.

He must see it. She could see it in him——he wanted to throw caution to the wind and make the most of the night. Take all the things they couldn't have, just one more time. Emma wanted that too.

But Josh was far too much of a gentleman, too nice a guy, to press her. He nodded, putting the library key into his pocket, and started to walk back through the conservatory.

'Josh!'

He turned. 'You're right, Em. It's been a great week, and I really hope that it's laid the foundations for us to meet up again sometime. But right now, we have to get on with our lives.'

'Tomorrow. We have to get on with our lives tomorrow. And we both know that, so it's not as if we'd be making any promises that can be broken.'

Josh was staring at her. Emma knew exactly what she wanted, and she knew what he wanted too. Maybe they could both learn to deal with parting a little better.

'Our last goodbye…' She shrugged uncomfortably. 'It was bitter. I left and I was determined on never seeing you again. We could do much, much better than that, this time.'

He still hesitated. 'It's not the traditional way of saying goodbye to someone.'

'Who cares? All that matters is whether it works for us, and we want it to happen.'

His eyes softened. In the presence of those eyes it was impossible that tonight could end now.

'Never be in any doubt that it's what I want, Em.'

No more words. He went to fetch their coats

and closed the front door behind them in silence. It was ten minutes' walk to Josh's mews apartment, but hardly a word passed between them. His arm around her waist, and way his body moved in perfect harmony with hers when he shortened his long stride, was enough.

The quiet cobbled mews was just the same, and so was Josh's apartment. Emma took his hand, leading him up the staircase that ran from the ground-floor garage up to the open-plan living area. And then the second flight, which led to his bedroom.

'You're sure, Em?' His fingers caressed the side of her cheek. 'I could make you cocoa, and show you to the spare room...'

'You want that?' Emma stood on her toes, kissing his mouth.

'No.'

'Me neither.'

He backed her against the wall. Lifted her up, so that she could wind her arms around his shoulders, her legs around his hips. Josh specialised in long delicious nights, and he was clearly in no mood to miss a moment of this one. He kissed her and the long, slow dance began. Rediscovering each fine curve of his body. Feeling the ever-increasing wash of desire as he reacquainted himself with all the things that made her sigh with pleasure.

The bedroom was in darkness, their bodies silhouetted in the light from the streetlamps outside.

'I have to see you, Josh.' Not just an outline. Emma wanted to see the light in his eyes as he made love to her.

He chuckled, putting her down and reaching out to punch the switch that closed the curtains. A whirr sounded as the room was plunged into darkness, and then Emma blinked as he switched the light on.

'Better?'

'Much. You still have the seduction cave curtains, then?' The automatic curtains had been in the apartment when Josh had bought it, and they'd laughed over opening and closing the curtains with the control at the bedside.

'I do. Not that they've been getting any use for the purposes of seduction.' He bent to kiss her. 'In case you were wondering.'

She had been. It was beyond belief that Josh wouldn't have had anyone in the last three years, but she couldn't quite forget the *out of practice* comment he'd made when they'd kissed in Brighton.

'So the last time for both of us was right here, then.' Forget the usual platitudes about wanting to move on and be happy. There had been no one else for either of them, and Josh clearly wanted to hear that as much as Emma did.

'Which makes me all the more hungry for you.' Their pace became more urgent as they both undressed and then Josh picked her up, laying her gently down onto the bed. 'All the more keen to make this last.'

That wasn't going to happen. Emma had had three years to think about all the things she missed about Josh, and to regret all of the things they'd never had a chance to do. She rolled him over onto his back, feeling in the drawer of the bedside cabinet.

The condoms were in exactly the same place. It might even be the same packet for all she knew; it looked like the ones they used to use. Josh propped himself up on his elbows, watching as she rolled the condom down and then straddled him.

'All for you, Josh. Just enjoy.'

He reached for her and she batted his hands away. When she sank down, taking him inside, he let out a sharp sigh.

'Emma... Wait, I can't...'

'You can't hold on? That's exactly what I want.' She moved her hips and he groaned. 'You like that?'

'What do you think?'

He liked it a lot. Josh liked it even better when she took the pins from her hair, shaking it free as she moved her hips in an ever-increasing rhythm.

'Em...' His body was shaking now. 'Please, Em, I need to feel you...'

She knew what that meant. He needed to feel her come, before he could let go. Usually he would make sure that she came more than once, in a long and delicious climb that robbed her of all control. It was Josh's turn to find out just how amazing that loss of everything felt.

And he was close. She leaned forward, finding just the right angle to please them both. Josh reached for her, and she caught his wrists, pressing them down against the mattress. She leaned forward to kiss him, and then straightened a little, cupping her breast in her hand.

'Emma... Em, please...'

Josh choked out the words and she came, hard, and without any warning at all. He must be able to see it and feel it, because suddenly he lost control, calling out for her again as his body jolted with a release that seemed to go far beyond pleasure. Far beyond anything they'd ever done together.

Josh had wanted tonight to be all for her, but Emma had purposely turned everything onto its head. This wasn't just a fond goodbye. It had the power to change everything.

She drew the covers of the bed over them and curled up in his arms. Maybe she was unaware of the fact that he'd lost control, but he very much doubted it. This one act had taken all of the hurt, all the hope and all the pleasure of the last week, and in a moment of world-rocking pleasure it had set him free.

'Are you done with me?' He kissed the top of her head.

'I don't think so.' Josh felt her fingers tracing small circles on his chest.

'Good. I'm not done with you yet either.'

Emma laughed lazily. 'You are for the time being, sweetheart.'

Yes and…no. He rolled her over, pulling her back against his stomach. When he wound his arm around her, one hand cupping her breast, the other sliding between her legs, Emma's sharp gasp told him that she still wanted him. She was going to want him even more in a minute…

'Maybe you'll beg,' he whispered in her ear, and she shivered against him.

'Like you did?'

'Yep. Just like that…'

CHAPTER NINE

IT HAD BEEN a long, delicious night. It was ironic that this one, last goodbye seemed to have freed them both to reach out for things that had eluded them before. But Emma was under no illusions. As soon as they tumbled out of bed, sleepy-headed and a little achy, the things that kept them apart would still be there. Josh would always want one kind of life, and Emma would always want another. And they'd always be limited by the things they feared.

It was past noon, and Josh had brought her coffee and toast, when her phone rang. Emma picked it up, pressing her fingers across her lips before answering it.

'Hi, David. I was going to call later and say thank you for last night. It was a lovely party.' Emma sat up in bed, automatically wrapping a sheet around her, despite the fact that Josh's father couldn't actually *see* what she was doing.

'Thank you for being there, Emma. Your presence made our evening.'

Always the charmer. Like father, like son. But David seemed to be a little more inclined to talk business this morning…or afternoon. Emma took another mouthful of coffee, trying to push herself out of the sleepy languor that was probably sounding in her voice.

'I've been speaking to a few colleagues about Iain Warner, the live liver transplant donor that you've been taking care of up in Liverpool. It should be going ahead any day now.'

'Yes? That's good. Val has everything sorted?' Iain had been attending St Agnes's Hospital in Liverpool for counselling before the transplant of a section of his liver went ahead, and Emma had carried out the medical checks that were needed, to make sure he was in good health.

'It's all arranged. As you know, Val's been working with Iain in Liverpool, and I've been working with the recipient and her family in London. The transplant co-ordinator at the London Metropolitan Hospital has been off sick, and it was envisaged that Val and I would be liaising over the donor and recipient's respective needs. But now that Val's handed in her notice at St Agnes, they'd prefer she spends as much time as possible with her replacement. I'm also hoping to make my involvement rather less hands-on…'

David was keeping the promise he'd made to

Val. Of course he was. 'What can I do to help, David?'

'I was wondering if you might spend some time at the London Metropolitan Hospital, overseeing the medical and pastoral needs of both donor and recipient and liaising between the two teams. Val and I will both be available if you have any questions or concerns, and if you're agreeable I can square things with St Agnes. As Josh will be the surgeon for the recipient's team, you'll be working closely with him as well.'

Emma swallowed hard. This was a senior position, one which she hadn't expected to be offered for a few years. It was only for two weeks, but it would be really valuable experience.

And she'd be working closely with the guy she'd just been saying *goodbye* to. All night. In the most incredible way possible.

'Have you spoken with Josh about this?'

'I wanted to speak with you first. It'll be a challenging two weeks for you, but I wouldn't give you this opportunity if I didn't think you could do it. And in case you think that I'm pulling strings, I'll mention that Dr Khan spoke to me the other day. I know you haven't been at St Agnes's Hospital for very long, but he's very impressed with your work already and he asked me if I might suggest some opportunities that would broaden your experience.'

Dr Khan had said *that*? The head of the Transplant Unit at St Agnes's rationed out his praise sparingly, but everyone knew that a *well done* from him was worth a great deal. And since Josh was sitting right next to her, then he couldn't possibly think that this was something she'd sought out, just to postpone the moment of parting.

'What's your answer, Emma?' David prompted her gently.

'I... Thank you. I'd love to be involved with this case and... I'll do my very best to make everything go smoothly. As long as Josh is happy with it.'

'Why wouldn't he be? And your best is always good enough, Emma. Don't forget that I'm only a phone call away, and I'll expect regular updates from you.' A voice sounded in the background. 'And Val sends her love.'

Despite herself, Emma smiled. It was nice to hear David's softer side reflected in his voice when he spoke Val's name.

'Give her my love, David. And thank you. This is a really exciting opportunity.'

'I'm glad you think so. Val and I will be driving up to Liverpool this afternoon, and so we'll see you tomorrow. In the meantime, I'll speak with Josh.'

A sudden moment of panic swept over Emma. Did David somehow know where she was? But then David ended the call, and Emma laid the phone down in front of her, on the bed.

'What did Dad want? And why do I need to be happy with it?' She felt Josh's hand on her spine, and shivered. How was she going to tell him?

'I...um... He...'

The sound of Josh's phone saved her the trouble. He looked at the display, and grinned. 'Looks as if he can tell me himself.'

Josh didn't spend a great deal of time in his office. It was quiet and comfortable, and being on the fourteenth floor it had a great view, right across the centre of London. But on the whole, he preferred to be either in the operating theatre or on the wards. Shutting himself away in here seemed like time wasted to him.

But today, it was where he needed to be. His conversation with David had convinced him that this was a great opportunity for Emma, and that she should grab it with both hands. It was awkward that it should come so soon after what was supposed to be a fond goodbye—*very* awkward, actually, since that night had felt a lot like the start of something and not the end—but Josh was just going to have to deal with it.

Emma's first reaction had been much the same as his. She'd jumped out of bed as soon as he'd ended his call with David, and he'd shouted his own approval of the arrangement through the door of the shower. She'd come out pink-faced and a little jittery, grabbing a towel to wrap around her before she kissed him. One moment of stillness, in warm remembrance of their night together, and then they were both on the move again. Josh had thrown on a pair of jeans and a sweatshirt, and Emma had twisted her hair into a tight plait without even bothering to dry it. He'd driven her back to her hotel and remembered to mention that he was looking forward to seeing her again and working with her. One last kiss and she was gone, saying that she would email him and let him know when she'd be arriving back in London.

When her email came, it gave her ETA as nine a.m. on Thursday. Clearly she wasn't planning on popping in for cocktails, or anything else, as soon as she got to London the night before. She was setting the tone for the next two weeks, and Josh was grateful for that.

She arrived at two minutes to nine, carrying a briefcase and two cups of coffee. He pushed the wastepaper bin, where he'd just thrown his empty coffee cup, under the desk with his foot.

'Coffee. You're a lifesaver.'

Emma smiled. She was dressed for business, in dark trousers and a white shirt, her hair tied back in a fishtail plait. Not quite as much fun as her sixties minidresses, but Josh wasn't sure that he'd be able to concentrate on anything else if she turned up in one of them.

She put the coffee down on his desk and sat down in one of the visitors' chairs, bending to open her briefcase and drawing out a thick file. Josh could sense that beneath her air of calm, she was nervous. He was nervous too…

'Good trip down?'

'Yes, thanks. I decided to get the train.'

No red Mini in the hospital car park, then. 'Where are you staying?'

Her cheeks reddened slightly. 'A hotel in Battersea.'

'Comfortable?'

'It's fine. I'm not planning on being there all that much.'

Uncomfortable, then, but presumably cheap. Josh would have offered her his spare room, but that would be a step too far for both of them.

'This is…'

Emma nodded. 'Awkward.'

'Yes.' The room seemed suddenly very quiet as well.

'What do you say we run through some preliminary details, if you have time?' Emma smiled suddenly. 'It's somewhere to start.'

Josh peeled the plastic lid from his coffee cup. 'Yeah. That sounds good.'

'Okay. The donor has been attending St Agnes's Hospital for counselling and tests. He's twenty-eight years old and teaches at the university. His family are all in London so he'll have good support after the operation. He's also in very good health—try as we might, we can't find anything wrong with him.'

'Good.' The procedure was actually more risky for the donor than for the recipient in these kinds of transplant, and there was a whole barrage of tests to be done before the transplant could go ahead. 'And he's not related to our recipient.'

'No. He joined the organ donation register about a year ago, and our counsellor is satisfied that he knows the risks and that this is what he wants to do.' Emma paused to take a sip of her coffee.

Josh knew that this was all Emma would be telling him about the donor, because donor and recipient each had separate medical teams, so that they could make decisions about the welfare of each patient without any conflict of interest. Donor and recipient were also kept apart, as a matter of course, and Emma was one of the few people who would have access to both of them and all their medical notes. She could also call on the resources of the GDK Foundation if they were needed.

It was the difficult job his father did, involving discretion, balance and medical knowledge. Emma would have access to David's expertise and judgement, but it would stretch anyone. Josh was proud that his father had chosen so well.

'David's given me all the notes for the recipient, but I'd like to hear your thoughts.'

Josh nodded. 'She's a seven-year-old girl, who developed cholestasis as a baby due to an infection. There was a delay in getting medical help for her, as her birth mother was a drug addict who wasn't capable of looking after her daughter and subsequently gave her up for adoption. She was very seriously ill for some time and it took a lot of hard work to keep her liver from failing. It was permanently damaged though and she's now at a stage where she needs a transplant.'

'And there was no blood type match from her adoptive parents?'

'Nope. Or any of her adoptive family. Dad told me that he told her parents that anyone in the family who'd like to consider donation could come to his office for immediate testing and fourteen people turned up the following morning. But Amy's O Negative and none of them were a match, so her only chance is an unrelated donor.' Josh shrugged. All that mattered was in the notes, but there was more. 'And she's a good kid.'

Emma smiled suddenly. 'I can't wait to meet her. You'll be doing her surgery, and—' she consulted her notes '—Mr Sargent will be responsible for the donor's surgery?'

'That's right. Alex Sargent's one of the best surgeons I've ever met, and we've done a lot of these types of cases before. If I have time I usually pop in to the viewing gallery for the donor's surgery, just so that I can see if there are any issues I should be aware of.' He risked a smile. 'Will you be joining me?'

'Yes, I'd like to. Thank you.' Emma had a long list in front of her, the text too small to read at this distance and upside down, but her pencil hovered over one of the entries. Josh congratulated himself on answering the question before it was asked.

There were, however, plenty of other items on her list, and Emma had many other questions. Some of them were obviously at David's instigation, but others had a flair and thoroughness that were entirely Emma. She'd taken David's advice, but it was obvious that Emma was doing this her way too.

After half an hour, she ran out of questions, which was just as well because Josh had run out of answers. Emma drained what was left in her coffee cup and flipped her file closed.

'That's it, then.' Her expression told him that it wasn't it at all. There was one more pressing challenge that they both had to face.

'Josh, I... I know that things haven't worked out quite the way that we intended. I hope you're okay with that.'

He'd better stick with what they'd originally intended, because Josh was still struggling with what had actually happened. The way he'd given himself to her, and how over the last couple of days he hadn't been able to take anything back.

'We intended to draw a line under what happened between us, so that we could move forward. This feels like moving forward to me.'

'And to me. Thank you.' She gave him a gorgeous smile. The one he loved and would tell any number of lies for. He could pretend that he didn't want her every time he saw her if this was his reward.

'I have to go. I have a surgery this morning.' A thought occurred to him. 'Have they given you somewhere to work? You can take my office if you like. I won't be needing it for the rest of the day.'

Emma hesitated. 'They said they'd find me a desk in the main office...'

Right. No one here would have dared suggest that David take a desk in the main office. Emma may not be as senior as him, but part of her role here was to act as his representative. And in the complex politics of any large institution, nothing screamed *important* quite as much as someone's work space.

'I insist.' He rounded the desk, risking the contact required to propel her towards his chair. Emma gave a small yelp of alarm, but when she sat down she seemed more comfortable with the arrangement.

'Make yourself at home. I'll be back later.' Josh turned on his heel, ignoring her thanks, and walked out of the room.

Emma had spent the day familiarising herself with the hospital and speaking to everyone on the two medical teams. It was a wide range of people, nurses and medical doctors, surgical teams, physiotherapists and counsellors. But she was beginning to get the measure of everyone, and David had told her that this was the first thing she needed to do. Learn the process and learn the people.

At six o'clock, Josh popped his head around the door. 'Just getting my coat...'

'Come in. This is actually *your* office.'

'Hmm.' He looked around. 'Like what you've done with the place.'

She'd touched nothing. There was only a small tube of hand cream on the desk, from when she'd last washed her hands. Emma snatched it up and dropped it into her bag. But Josh seemed relaxed and cheerful and a day of activity had left her feeling less nervous and embarrassed too.

'Are you wondering how my day went?'

'Thought you'd never ask.' He grinned, lowering himself into one of the visitors' chairs. 'How did your day go?'

'Good. I managed to talk with everyone. I think everything's under control.'

In control. The words had just slipped out and she'd seen the warmth bloom in Josh's eyes. He'd told her how much he liked that, and she'd seen what had happened when he'd lost control. It had been earth-shattering.

And it had been a goodbye. Something that moved them on to a new stage in their relationship, and which couldn't be done again, however much Emma wanted it. Ached for it, every time she saw Josh.

'So, do you fancy a coffee? You can pay.'

Emma chuckled. Josh's easy-going humour had a way of cutting through awkward moments.

'I could murder a coffee. I've been talking all day.'

CHAPTER TEN

EMMA HAD WONDERED whether Josh might suggest that they meet up at the weekend and wondered what her answer would be. But he'd saved her the trouble of having to grapple with that particular problem, by acting like a friend instead of a lover, and saying he'd see her on Monday morning.

She spent another night in an uncomfortable bed, listening to the loud hum of traffic outside her window. There had been so much to do that she'd booked the first hotel on the list of places to stay, and breakfast had confirmed her opinion that she really ought to try and move somewhere a little more comfortable. Emma headed into the hospital, deciding that it was the only place where she'd get some peace and quiet to find somewhere else and also get some work done.

She found Josh's office unlocked, and when she opened the door he was sitting at his desk.

'Oh... Sorry, I didn't know you'd be here today.'

'That's all right.' He jumped to his feet. 'I just

popped in. I'll get out of your way. You're working today?'

'I just popped in too. I'll be here tomorrow as well, to make sure that the donor gets settled and that there are no issues.'

Josh nodded. 'Yeah, good thought. I'll…um…'

He fell silent. One of those silences that spoke volumes. He looked tired and his brow was creased with worry.

'What's up? One of your patients?'

He shook his head.

'What, then?' Josh didn't answer, and Emma decided to take another tack. 'Have you had breakfast?'

'Uh? No.'

'Well, I hear there's a place around the corner that does a great breakfast. I could do with something more than a piece of limp toast and a cup of weak tea, so you'll be doing me a favour. I'm hoping for almond croissants, preferably still warm, although I think I'll take almost anything.'

Josh smiled suddenly. 'You mean Riley's? Yeah, everyone goes there. I think they do almond croissants…'

'You're getting my hopes up now.' She chivvied him to his feet. 'Come on…'

Riley's did indeed do almond croissants. And hot chocolate. Emma ordered two of everything, and Josh carried their plates to a table in the corner.

'Is this the Dr Owen care package?' He sat down, stretching his shoulders as if they ached.

'That's far too organised for me. Call it a friendly ultimatum. If you don't tell me what's up by the time I've finished this croissant, then I'm just going to keep ordering until you do.'

He gave her a long look. 'You're in not-at-work mode, aren't you?'

'I wasn't aware of transforming suddenly as I left the building.' Emma considered the idea. 'I guess I've been trying pretty hard to get everything right.'

Trying to be friendly but not too friendly. Walking that thin line, when all of her instincts were trying to push her off balance and back to a place where she was falling in love with him all over again. But Josh looked as if he needed a friend right now.

'It wasn't intended as a criticism. I like both your different personas.'

Emma leaned across the table, towards him. 'Then you should know that both of them are asking the same question. What's up?'

Josh took a deep breath. 'You know I told you that I had no contact with my biological family? Well, I got an email last night.'

'From who?'

'My biological father got married again after he and Mum divorced. The email was from one of his sons.'

'You mean your half-brother?'

'Yeah. Suppose so.' Josh seemed to be turning the idea over in his head. 'Seems a bit weird having a brother, even if he is only half a brother.'

He didn't seem overjoyed about it all. Emma could see that he must have conflicting feelings. 'And how do you feel about that?'

'I feel...pleased. He said he'd like to meet me and I'd like to meet him.'

'That's a good start, then, isn't it?'

Josh shook his head. 'I don't know. I keep wondering how Dad's going to feel about it all.'

Emma thought for a moment. 'I guess that David must always have known this was a possibility. He must have thought about it. Has he ever mentioned you getting in touch with your biological family before?'

'Once or twice. I always told him I didn't need to. But now...' Josh shook his head. 'His name's Jamie. Knowing that I have a half-brother, and that he has a name, makes it all seem a bit more real. As if my biological family isn't just an idea that I can dismiss.'

'You want to hear what I really think?' This was so personal that Emma hardly dared give an opinion.

'Nah. If you could just fob me off with a few platitudes, then I'm sure I'll feel a great deal better about things.' Josh grinned suddenly. 'Of course I want to hear what you think; it's why I caved in to the intolerable pressure you were applying.'

He was joking. But Emma had come to understand that Josh's jokes were capable of covering a whole world of hurt.

'I think you need to talk to David. Tell him what's happened and ask him how he feels.'

'I don't know whether I can. Maybe I should just say nothing.'

'And how do you think he'll feel if you do that? Josh, I think this is the first time I've ever heard you say that you can't talk to your father about anything.'

'It's the first time I've ever felt it. Apart from when I was a kid, and deciding to run away from home, but that's a long time ago, now.'

'You ran away because you were afraid David didn't want you?'

Josh nodded.

'I know you're really happy for him and Val, but…be honest. Has it occurred to you that his getting married or you getting back in touch with your biological family are things that might make him want you a little less?'

'No, I…' Josh answered quickly and then

stopped to think for a moment. 'Maybe. Not in so many words, but it really touched a nerve when you said it. I can't discount the idea.'

'Should I just leave that with you?' Emma didn't want to press him too hard.

'Yeah.' He grabbed his hot chocolate, taking a sip. 'So what are you up to today? You have work to do?'

'Not really. To be honest, the hotel's a bit bleak and I reckoned I might as well come into the hospital.'

'Nothing else to do? What's got into you?'

Emma laughed. 'It's not serious. Just a twenty-four-hour thing, I'll be better in the morning.'

'Fancy a day out? Bettering ourselves?'

It was an old joke. They'd take the train into the centre of London and wander around museums and galleries. No plan, no direction, just taking everything as it came and appreciating whatever was in front of them.

'Why not? I haven't done that in a while.'

They found their way to the Victoria and Albert Museum. It was one of the places that Emma liked getting lost in the most, a celebration of the eclectic where it was never possible to be quite sure what was around the next corner. They'd wandered for hours, and then Josh had taken his phone from his pocket.

'I have a call to make. Do you mind?'

Emma knew who he'd be calling. 'Go. I'll meet you by the Exhibition Road entrance in…half an hour?'

'It shouldn't take that long.'

'Yes, it should. Three-quarters of an hour for good measure.'

Josh grinned. 'I'll go now before you make it an hour.'

Wandering wasn't quite so relaxing when you were looking at your watch every two minutes, but Emma stuck to her word. Forty-five minutes later, she walked back through the galleries, and out into the traffic-free zone outside the museum. Josh was sitting alone on a bench.

He seemed *very* alone, staring at his phone, obviously deep in thought. Emma walked over to him, sitting down next to him. Putting her hand on his shoulder seemed the obvious thing to do, and he looked up at her.

'So?'

'Dad's good with it all. He says that it's entirely up to me, but he'll back me all the way if I want to meet up with Jamie.'

So it was *Jamie* now. David had obviously put Josh's mind at rest.

'Did he know about your biological father's family?'

'He said that Mum tried to get in touch with

him. She didn't much want to but she felt it would be good to at least know where he was in case I ever wanted to meet him. She sent a couple of letters but they went unanswered.'

'So…that means they at least thought about the possibility.'

'Dad says he's sending me something.' His phone beeped and Josh glanced down at it. 'Here it is.'

Maybe this was for Josh alone to see. Emma drew back, turning her head up towards the people strolling past them, then felt Josh nudge her.

'Here. You know the picture I have of the river, in my study?'

'Yes? I've always liked it.'

Josh grinned. 'That was the last birthday card my mum gave me. It's her own work.'

'She was very talented.' The watercolour of the Thames was brimming with life and colour.

'Dad keeps a scan of what she wrote inside, framed in his study. He says it's a reminder for him.' Josh handed the phone to her, and she saw three neatly written lines.

'Green ink. I like her style.' Emma smiled.

'Yeah, that's Mum all over. She used to write letters of complaint in red ink.'

'Even better.' Emma turned the phone, enlarging the image as much as the small screen would allow, and held it between them.

So close. A little too close for comfort but… comfort was just what Josh needed at the moment. Emma read the inscription carefully.

Remember always that you can take whatever you want from life, Josh. And that, however far you travel, David and I will always be here for you.

'That's nice.' Unbearably sad too, because Josh's mother hadn't lived to see him leave the nest.

'Yeah. Dad kept her promise for her.' Josh looked up at Emma, and she brushed the tear away from her cheek.

'So are you any closer to deciding what you want to do?'

'I'm going to write to Jamie and tell him I'd like to meet up with him. Dad's all for the idea.'

'That's good. David's reassured you, then?'

'He tells me that I'm welcome to run away again, any time I like, because he's got a little project in mind to surprise Val with and he could do with the extra pair of hands. He's making her a vegetable garden at the house in Oxford.'

'She'll like that.' Josh had taken Emma to David's house in Oxford when they'd first met. It felt about a million years ago, now. It was large and beautiful, with plenty of land at the back to grow whatever food supplies Val set her heart on.

'Will she? I told Dad that a rose garden might be a little bit more appropriate.'

'Not for Val. She likes growing things you can eat.'

'In that case I may have to dispense with the running away part and go down there anyway to help him with the digging.' Josh stretched his arms out, as if readying them for the task. But it seemed a weight had been lifted from his shoulders.

'This hotel of yours. Is it really that bad?' he asked.

'It's really noisy. I'm not getting any sleep, so I think I'll have to find somewhere else. I was in a rush when I booked it and I just took the first place on the list.'

Josh nodded. 'I don't suppose you'd consider staying at mine for a few nights? Solely in the interests of a productive working day. Take the spare room, or the sofa…or you could even go down to the garage and sleep in the car if you're reckoning on a quick getaway.'

'In case David phones, you mean?'

He nodded. 'Yeah. If he does that again, I think we should at least take the time to have breakfast.'

'Breakfast would be great. And I could do with an undisturbed night's sleep as well.'

'I'm your man, then. We can go back to mine to pick up the car, and then drive down to Battersea to get your luggage. We'll get something for dinner on the way back; my fridge is startlingly empty at the moment.'

Josh was planning again. Those plans didn't seem quite so restrictive now, just a way of fitting everything into the day. 'Okay. Thanks, that sounds really good.'

Josh felt…complete. Not just because of Jamie's email, or his father's reaction to it. Because Emma had been there, and she seemed happy to be doing all the things they'd done once upon a time, when he'd thought that he could map their future out together.

There were no maps, now. No navigation along a well-charted route. But that was okay, because worrying about tomorrow was how he'd lost Emma. She was here now, and he had to get used to the fact that she'd be finding another place to stay soon, and that she'd be gone.

Emma had insisted on cooking, and Josh had sat down to write his email to Jamie. He'd written a few versions, some of which were exactly the same apart from the location of the commas, before Emma made him put his deliberations to one side and come and eat.

When they'd finished, he put on some music and asked her to look at the latest incarnation of his email, and they sat on the sofa together while Emma read it carefully. She suggested that *I'd like to meet* might be injected with a little more enthusiasm, and that *I'd love to meet* might be better. Josh found that a little too gushy, and they compromised at *I'd very much like to meet.*

He pressed 'send' and they both stared at the screen. Just assuming that the email had left the building, in the same way that he usually did, didn't seem quite enough.

'Has it gone? I didn't hear anything.' Emma was clearly thinking the same.

Josh opened his 'sent' folder. 'Yes. It's gone.'

'Good.' She reached over, closing his laptop. 'It might be a while before he gets back to you. He must be getting used to all of this becoming a reality as well.'

'Yeah. He's only twenty and…' Josh thought for a moment. 'I'm not entirely sure what big brothers are supposed to do.'

'What you're doing now. Be a bit protective, but give him plenty of space. Listen to what he wants and tell him how you feel.'

'In other words, juggle.' Perhaps Emma could

advise on that, because she seemed to do it a lot better than he could. 'Anything else?'

She rolled her eyes. 'How am I supposed to know? I don't have any brothers. Just be yourself, Josh. That's what he wants out of this. He said it in his email; he just wants to get to know you.'

'Fair enough.' He could think about the ramifications of that later. When his whole consciousness wasn't bound up with having Emma close. 'You fancy a film?'

'That sounds good. What have you got?'

'Whatever you want.' Josh handed her the remote for the TV and went to inspect the contents of the freezer for dessert. 'Vanilla or raspberry? Or… I think this is strawberry.' He inspected the canister of home-made ice cream.

'You've been making your own ice cream?' Emma was flipping through the list of films on the TV screen.

'Gran bought me an ice cream maker for Christmas.'

'Really?' Emma's eyebrows shot up in surprise.

'Yeah, she's got a bit of a scatter-gun approach to present buying sometimes.' Josh decided not to mention that Gran had included a note, which said that one of the best ways to any woman's heart was to feed her home-made ice cream, and that she hoped her gift might rectify the noticeable lull in his love life over the past few years.

'Let's not disappoint her, then. I'll have the strawberry. Is it pink?'

'Very...' The ice cream looked slightly too pink, but when Josh took a taste of it, it wasn't too bad. 'Definitely strawberry, I think I may have added a few too many.'

'You can *never* have too many strawberries, Josh.' She dropped the remote on the sofa and jumped to her feet. 'Let me have a taste.'

Josh fetched another spoon from the drawer, and she leaned across the counter that divided the kitchen from the living space, taking a sample from the tub.

'Mmm...' Emma grimaced. 'I hate to say it, because I so wanted to like your gran's pink ice cream. But this is too sweet. You put sugar in as well?'

'Yeah. It's not so bad, is it?'

'You always did have a sweeter tooth than me.'

'So you'll have—?' *Raspberry.* He was going to say raspberry, but Emma had leaned over a little further and kissed him. And now he was caught in her spell, unable to think of anything else.

'Emma...' She'd kissed him, so it was only fair to kiss her back. Quid pro quo.

But that was a slippery slope and he was skid-

ding down it now. A caress of her fingertips...
Another kiss that was all the sweeter because he
couldn't pull her close and the sensation on his
lips seemed so much more in focus...

'Em, I didn't intend on this happening.'

'Neither did I.'

And yet it had. She slid up onto the counter,
swinging her legs over in one smooth move. Josh
hooked his hands behind her knees, pulling her
forward until their bodies touched and he heard
her catch her breath.

One more heartbeat, and he would be completely lost. But he had to know.

'Are you sure, Em?'

'Unfair question.' She kissed him again, her
eyes dark with desire. For all he knew her judgement was just as clouded as his was at the moment.

It took a supreme effort of will to back away
from her. 'I really need you to be sure, Emma.'

The moment was slipping away, but it would
take one look, just one kiss, to get it back. And
just one word from Emma to make them friends
again, ones who stayed the night in separate bed-
rooms.

'We're a good team. Great in bed...' She gave
him a wicked smile.

'I'd say a lot better than great.' Josh grinned
back, wondering where this was going.

'We just want different things, and we're afraid of what that means. So why don't we just stick to what we're good at, no promises, no looking forward? Just putting the past to rest.'

'Write our own rules?'

'Why not, Josh? Life's going to happen whatever we do, so we may as well do what we both want to.'

He walked towards her, planting his hands on the countertop on either side of her hips. 'Rule one. You should kiss me, now.'

Emma smiled and the moment was back. Better because his head was clear now, and he knew hers was too. She kissed him and the next moment seemed to rush in on them, impatiently.

'Rule two.' Her hand tugged at his shirt. 'Take it off…'

CHAPTER ELEVEN

EMMA HAD LOST COUNT. Numbers didn't matter in Josh's arms and neither did rules, because there *were* no rules to his brand of seduction. Just a slow, delicious appreciation of every moment. Half their clothes were scattered downstairs, and the other half tangled together beside the bed.

He lay her down, his steady rhythm propelling her on, like an unstoppable tide. She came almost straight away, feeling him harden inside her in response.

Maybe it was these new rules that were making her feel this way. Free to be loved by him, and free to love him back. Josh seemed different too, more ragged and unpredictable. He'd always been a tender man—he couldn't change that if he tried—but there was an edge of the exciting unknown in his lovemaking tonight.

'You adore this as much as I do?'

He smiled down at her. One arm was wrapped around her shoulders, and she felt his other hand on her leg, pulling it up a little so they could feel just that bit more of each other.

'Maybe *more* than you do...' He moved again, sending bright showers of feeling through her body.

'Not possible, Josh.' She clung to him, his pleasure feeding hers.

He bent, whispering in her ear. 'You're making a competition of this?'

'Yes, I'm making a competition of it.' Josh always had been able to inflame her imagination and now the effect was head spinning.

Her fingers found the pulse on his neck, and the quickening beat of his heart lent yet another strand of pleasure. The rhythm of their lovemaking stepped up a notch, and there were no words now. Just that sweet, sweet feeling that something was waiting for them, and that when it came there would be no stopping it.

When it *did* come, there was a kind of madness to it. A rippling, insistent rapture that spread right to her fingertips. It was only then that he too lost control, crying out in agonised pleasure.

They held each other tight for a long time, their bodies still sensitive and vulnerable. And Josh was still perfect. In the quiet end to a day that had changed so much, Emma felt his body curl around hers, as she drifted off to sleep.

* * *

Emma was standing in front of the mirror, at the top of the stairs that led down to the front door, plaiting her red hair. Josh was supposed to be making coffee, but in truth he was watching her.

He'd found that place she went to, when she lost all control and just let the storm take her. It was a little frightening in its intensity, but the more he went there, the more he wanted to go back. When he'd woken in the night, and heard her whisper, 'Are you awake?' he'd gone from zero to a hundred and ten per cent in less time that it took him to reply.

Maybe it was because the rules had changed. Emma had laughingly referred to them this morning and he guessed that they both thought that had something to do with it.

'I've got to go into work today too.' Now that she'd worked her way down to the end of the plait and fastened it, Josh could pour the coffee without spilling all over the countertop.

'You do? What are you up to?'

'Amy wants to see the operating theatre, and her parents asked me if that would be possible. I had a few concerns, largely on the basis that it might frighten her. But I've been thinking about it and Amy's been around hospitals all her life and she has a different attitude than most kids might. She wants to know.'

Emma nodded. Josh pushed her coffee across the countertop towards her and waited for her reply. But she just took a sip of her coffee, her brow creasing slightly.

'I'm going to see her mother today and I thought I'd tell her that I'll take Amy up to the viewing gallery. What are your thoughts?' Josh would be very surprised if Emma didn't have any.

'Um… Yes.'

'Just *yes*?'

'I… It's difficult, Josh. You want me to disagree with you over this, when we spent last night doing…what we did.'

Maybe growing up with David had made Josh a bit more comfortable with breakfast conversations about surgery. But he suspected that Emma's reservations were a bit more complicated than that.

'Do you regret last night?' Guilt stabbed at him. Maybe he should have emphasised the need for them both to be very sure about this a bit more, but he thought he'd made it clear.

She seemed to be reading his mind. Emma reached across the counter, laying her hand on the side of his face. 'No regrets, Josh. I was sure then, and I'm even more sure now. Have you got that?'

'Got it. So what's the problem? Boundaries?' It was something that most people seemed to negotiate successfully. The nature of the work meant that there were plenty of couples amongst the staff at the hospital. Emma had never had any difficulties about drawing a line between working with David and starting up a relationship with Josh when they'd first met.

'It'… I want to make my mark, but I don't want to step on anyone's toes. And yes, boundaries are something I'm aware of, because I'm new at the hospital and I'm still finding my feet.'

'Okay, I appreciate that. So…perhaps we have a dress code. When your hair's tied back we're work colleagues. When it's not, then we can be friends. And…'

'When I take off my clothes…?' Emma grinned wickedly.

'Yeah, that's it. That includes when I take your clothes off for you as well.'

'Of course. Goes without saying.'

Josh wrenched his thoughts back on to the problem in hand. 'And whatever our state of dress, I'd appreciate it if you'd tell me what's on your mind. Because if you hold back on giving me your opinion on anything, then I'm going to have to sit you down and ask who you are, and what you've done with the Emma that I know.'

She grinned, reaching across the counter, with the obvious intention of kissing him. Josh ducked out of the way, backing off.

'Uh-uh. That's not in the agreement.' He teased her. 'Hair…'

'All right, then. About Amy…' Emma considered the matter for a moment. 'I think that if it's what she wants, then you should listen to her. One of her parents will be there, I assume.'

'Of course. Her mother probably.'

'Then she'll have plenty of support. And she's probably got some idea of what an operating theatre looks like anyway, as she may well have seen one on television. The real thing might come as a bit of a disappointment.'

Josh nodded. 'That's true. I hope she doesn't think I'm going to whip out a scalpel and do a demonstration.'

Emma laughed. 'I think the thing you really need to worry about is if she decides she wants to try some surgery out for herself. Little girls aren't all sugar and spice, you know. What time do you have to be there to see her mum?'

'Not until this afternoon. But I'll come in with you this morning. I can always find something useful to occupy my time.'

'The donor is going to be checking in this morning, and I said I'd come and see how he was settling in this afternoon.'

'Okay. Well, we could stay here until lunchtime, and review anything that's outstanding.'

'I've nothing outstanding. You?'

He wished that Emma wouldn't smile at him that way when she was dressed for work. 'Nope.'

'So what's the rule for having my hair up and no clothes?' Emma started to unbutton her blouse.

Josh smiled, leaning back against the kitchen counter. Maybe she was going to let him watch her undress; he'd like that a lot. 'No idea. You tell me.'

Josh was as good as his word. When they walked into the hospital together, he was smiling but professional and it was easy to be the same with him.

'Would you like to come along and meet Amy? I'm going to take her mum for coffee first, so we can wait for you while you see the donor.'

'Yes, thanks. I'll text you?'

Josh nodded. 'Perfect. See you later.' He walked away without looking back, and even though her hair was fixed neatly again at the back of her head, Emma allowed herself to watch.

The wards in the Transplant Unit were all split into single rooms, and Emma found Iain Warner sitting on the bed, reading a book.

'Hey, Emma.'

'Hi. What's the book for today?' Iain usually turned up to the hospital with a book under his arm, and joked that he'd read his way through the process of preparing for a liver donation.

'This is on the syllabus for my students, next term.' He turned the corners of his mouth down. 'I thought I'd have a chance to get my teeth into it, but it's not really happening.'

Emma picked up the book, looking at the blurb on the back cover. 'It looks pretty scholarly.'

'I thought that having something to concentrate on might be good.' Iain shrugged. 'Hospitals aren't really the place to concentrate, are they?'

'Not if you're a patient. Leave the concentration part to me.'

'And the surgeon.'

'Yes, definitely. I met Mr Sargent the other day. I'm told he's the very best.'

'I heard that too. Not much of a sense of humour though…' Iain paused, grinning.

'All right, I'll bite. What makes you say that?'

'When I came down to London for a consultation with him last week, he told me that the nature of this particular procedure meant I wouldn't have much of a scar. I said I'd rather there was, so I could impress my other half and that I had my eye on a scimitar-shaped one.'

Emma snorted with laughter. 'Don't. Where is Peter?'

'Gone to pick up my parents; he'll be back shortly. Can I ask you a favour?'

'Of course.'

'When I have the op…if anything goes wrong…'

'There's a very small chance of anything going wrong. But okay, if something does go wrong...'

'Will you talk to Peter, and tell him what's happening? Mr Sargent—he seems a good guy and he's obviously great at his job but Peter has a habit of asking for facts and figures when what he really needs is a kind but honest assessment. Which is what I reckon he'll get from you.'

It was a nice compliment. 'Thank you. I'll know how everything's gone as soon as your op is finished, so I can meet up with him while you're still in the recovery room. Give me his phone number.'

'Thanks. I appreciate it.' Iain reached over to the cabinet at the side of the bed for his phone. 'Coming atcha...'

The message popped up on Emma's screen and she saved the number. 'Got it. Tell him to expect my call.'

'I will do. Thanks.'

'Is there anything else I can do for you? I can go and see if the hospital shop has anything to read that's a bit lighter than that.' Emma pointed to the book on the bed.

'No, that's okay, thanks. I've saved some films on my tablet. I might give one of them a watch.' Iain thought for a moment, and Emma didn't move. Sometimes you had to wait a bit to hear the things people really wanted.

'You know there was a meeting, up in Liverpool? Me and the little girl's parents.'

'Yes, that's standard. We have to assess whether there have been any inducements or pressure on you to donate.'

'Yeah, I get that. But the one thing that struck me… The mother… I could see the pain in her eyes. But all the same, just as we were finishing up, she turned to me and told me that I had to be sure that this was what I really wanted to do.'

'She was right—you do have to be sure.'

Iain nodded. 'I get that too. But for her to say it, when she was obviously hoping against hope that I could help her little girl. It was generous, don't you think?'

'It takes one to know one, Iain. What you're doing is incredibly generous too.'

'I know it's against the rules and everything, but… I'd like her to know that I'm still sure.'

Emma took a moment to think. 'There isn't anything laid down in the regulations about donor recipient contact. We manage that on a case by case basis, and it's subject to everyone's wishes. What I can do is let the team dealing with your recipient know that there's a message and they'll do what they think is best for the family.'

'Yeah, that sounds good. Thanks.' Iain nodded his approval.

'On one condition.' Emma held her finger up

to emphasise the point. 'You're to stop worrying about everyone else. That's my job. You concentrate on yourself and your recovery, all right?'

'Yes, Doctor.'

Emma had waited with Iain until Peter returned with his parents, then texted Josh. He'd asked her to meet him outside the viewing gallery for Theatre Four, and after getting a complex set of directions from one of the nurses in the Transplant Unit, and making a couple of wrong turns, she finally found it.

Josh was standing with a woman and a little girl in a wheelchair. The yellow tone of her skin and sclera said that this must be Amy. Josh had clearly gone all out to make this experience as authentic as possible for Amy, and had changed into a pair of dark blue scrubs. They suited him far better than Emma could allow herself to contemplate while she was working, and she felt her heart thump as he turned his bright blue gaze on her.

'Ah, here she is.' Josh turned to the woman. 'This is Dr Emma Owen. She's taken over from David Kennedy. Emma, this is Julie Thompson, Amy's mum.'

'Hello. I'm sorry my husband isn't here to meet you. He's gone home to get some sleep.' Julie held out her hand to Emma. She was neatly dressed, her fair hair tied back in a curly ponytail, but the dark rings under her eyes showed the stress that she was under.

'I'm glad to have this opportunity to meet you and Amy.' Emma shook Julie's hand, then bent down towards Amy. 'Hi, Amy. I'm Emma.'

Amy looked at her steadily, clearly wondering who she was and why she was here.

'Dr Emma works with Dr David. She's got everything under control,' Josh volunteered, and Amy nodded, clearly impressed.

'Can we go inside, now?' She looked up at Josh.

'Yes, we can. We can't go into the operating theatre itself, but we can see everything from the gallery.'

'That's where people watch.' Amy turned to her mother to impart the extra information and then looked back up at Josh. 'Is someone going to watch *my* operation?'

'Not if you don't want them to,' Josh replied.

'I don't mind. I've seen it on TV—they watch and learn how to do it. You could show them, couldn't you?'

'No, I'm there just for you, no one else.' Josh had clearly seen Julie's alarmed expression.

'What about Mum and Dad? They could watch.'

A tear rolled down Julie's cheek at the thought,

and Josh squatted down in front of Amy. 'I've asked your mum and dad to wait outside, so that I can concentrate on doing my very best for you. But they'll be right here for you and they'll be the first people you see when you open your eyes.'

'Okay.' Amy leaned forward in her chair, putting her hand on Josh's knee. 'I trust you, Dr Josh.'

'Thank you, Amy.' Josh stood up suddenly, and Emma thought she saw him blink rapidly as he did so. 'So we'll go in now, shall we?'

Like so many seriously ill kids, Amy was older than her years. If everything went well tomorrow, then Josh would be restoring not just her health, but her childhood. All of her parents' hopes and fears rested on Josh's shoulders too, and Emma knew it was likely a heavy burden to carry.

But he did so lightly. Amy's wheelchair was placed at the centre of the curved viewing gallery, and her mother sat on one side, with Josh on the other. He explained everything and answered questions, and Emma saw that Julie was becoming more relaxed as he talked too.

'There's one more very important decision we need to make, Amy.' He reached for the bag he'd put on the empty seat next to him and drew out two scrub caps. 'Stars or stripes?'

Amy considered the question and Julie smiled

suddenly. 'What do you reckon, Amy? The stripes are colourful.'

'Ah. Your mum wants me to stick out in the crowd.' Josh chuckled.

'I like…stars.' Amy pointed at the dark blue cap with shooting stars on it. She was right, it would bring out the colour in Josh's eyes…

'Shooting stars it is, then, just for you. Now what do you say that you and your mum go and get a good night's sleep and I'll see you in the morning, eh?'

'Okay…' Amy seemed reluctant to go, and Emma caught Josh's eye, beckoning to him.

'All right, you can stay and look for just a few minutes, while I go and check something with Dr Emma.' He got to his feet, leaving Amy leaning forward to stare down into the operating theatre.

Emma quickly relayed Iain's message to him, and he nodded. 'What do you think?'

'You know Julie better than I do, and you're a senior member of Amy's team. It's your decision.'

'Okay. Will you sit with Amy while I take a couple of minutes to talk to Julie?'

'Sure. Thanks.'

Amy was tiring now, and she'd run out of questions to ask. Emma checked the drip that hung at the back of her wheelchair, smoothing the blanket that was tucked around her legs. Josh was standing with Julie at the back of the gallery, speaking quietly to her.

She saw Julie's hand fly to her mouth and she looked for a moment as if she was about to fall over. Josh put out his arm to steady her and she buried her face in his chest, her shoulders heaving with silent sobs. He produced a paper towel from his pocket, giving it to Julie, and she quietly dried her tears and blew her nose, listening to something that Josh was saying and nodding. It was a mime show of emotion, just one of the many that Julie must have had to keep from her daughter, and Emma's heart ached for her.

But Josh *had* made the right decision, because Julie was walking back down towards them, smiling broadly now. She sat down next to Amy, stroking her hair tenderly.

'Are you ready to go now, button?'

Amy nodded sleepily. Emma carefully manoeuvred the wheelchair past the line of seats, and out of the viewing gallery, and Julie walked beside her back to the paediatric transplant ward. Josh lifted Amy out of the wheelchair and into her bed, while Emma hooked the fluid bag back above her head, checking the drip chamber again to make sure that it was half full and properly regulating the fluids going into Amy's arm. Then a nurse came to shoo them away.

'See you tomorrow, Dr Josh,' Amy's voice sounded from the bed, and Josh turned quickly.

'See you tomorrow, Amy.'

Julie followed them out of the ward. 'Thank you, Josh. I really appreciate the time you've taken today. She'll sleep for an hour and then she'll be telling all the nurses about her visit to the operating theatre.'

'My pleasure. I hope it's helped her.'

'Yes, I think it has.' Julie turned to Emma. 'And thank you for the message. I don't know what to say in reply, there are so many things…'

'I think that just the fact it's been delivered will be enough. May I say that?'

'Yes, yes. And please…my heartfelt thanks as well.'

CHAPTER TWELVE

EMMA KNEW THE SIGNS. They'd gone to bed early, and Josh had slept soundly. He was up early, and when she got downstairs he'd made breakfast. A good night's sleep and a good breakfast was always the way when he had a long surgery scheduled.

But this time, she understood a little better. She'd always known that her job was a matter of meticulous care, over weeks and months, while his was an all-or-nothing turning point in his patients' lives. But she'd reckoned that Josh somehow distanced himself from his patients, as a way of coping with that. Seeing him with Amy had quashed that assumption completely.

How little they'd talked in those few months, caught up in a whirlwind romance that had never really found any solid ground before they'd argued so bitterly. There had been no professional contact, no real friendship, just an instinctive connection. So fragile that it was always destined to break, and when it had it had wounded them both, far more than Emma had ever anticipated.

'You're going up to see your donor?' he asked as they walked through the hospital reception together. Josh never mentioned Iain by name, and Emma knew this was his way of maintaining the separation between donor and recipient teams.

'Yes. You?'

'I'll be checking on Amy and then I'll sit in for a while in Theatre.'

'I'll probably see you there, then.'

He nodded, and they went their separate ways.

She found Iain sitting in a wheelchair, a little nervous but still determined. Peter was holding his hand tightly, smiling reassuringly.

'Emma. Could you get this guy off me? He's cutting off the circulation to my fingers.' Iain's bravado wasn't fooling anyone but himself.

'I think that they're about ready to go now anyway.' One of the nurses had just appeared in the doorway behind Emma.

Iain nodded. 'Right, then. Let's get this done, shall we?'

She'd walked down to the anaesthetic room, taking Peter's arm and leading him away when it was time to go. 'I'll wait here.' Peter pointed to a row of seats in the corridor outside.

'No, you won't. He isn't going to be coming out of that door, and you'll only be in the way.'

And Peter would be seeing a procession of one patient after another going into the theatre suite. That was enough to unsettle anyone.

'Okay…um…four hours, isn't it?'

'At least. It may be a little longer, but that's no indication of how things have gone.' That wasn't strictly true, and Emma hoped that it would be four hours at most. 'Would you like to go for a coffee?'

'No, probably not. I don't think so.'

'Okay, well, you know where the cafeteria is if you change your mind. What about some fresh air and stretching your legs for a while?'

'Yeah. That sounds good. You have my number, don't you?'

'I have it, and I'm going to be keeping tabs on exactly what's happening. I'll call you as soon as there's any news. Have you got my number?'

Peter took his phone from his pocket. 'No, I don't.'

His hand was shaking and Emma took the phone from him, putting her number into the memory. 'Call me any time you want. If I'm busy and can't answer I want you to leave a message, so that I can get straight back to you.'

'Thanks.' Peter let out a sigh. 'Iain and I have been together five years now and he's the bravest person I know. He's got this chance of changing some little kid's life and it's not something he's prepared to let go of.'

'What he's doing is amazing. What you're doing in supporting him is hard too, Peter. Hang on in there, because he's relying on you.'

Peter straightened suddenly. 'Thanks. I'll see you in four hours.'

The process was well choreographed. The right lobe of Iain's liver would be extracted, meanwhile Amy would be prepped for surgery. There would be a careful examination, to make sure that the liver section was viable, and it would be taken through to the adjoining operating theatre, where Josh would be waiting to make his first incision. While that was happening Alex Sargent would be finishing up, closing Iain's wound.

Emma found Josh sitting in the operating theatre viewing gallery watching as Alex operated. He was leaning forward, obviously deep in thought, and Emma sat down quietly beside him.

'Everything okay?' He didn't look around.

'Yes, fine.' Going into details would only break his concentration.

His terse comments were useful though. He clearly held Alex in high esteem as a surgeon, and he was nodding his head in approval of the way things were going. He didn't need to explain anything to her, but the finer points of the keyhole incision were interesting, along with the way he read what was going on. When Alex turned, holding up his hand to the gallery windows, he stood up.

'That's my invitation to leave.'

Emma nodded. They both had their parts to play; Josh knew she'd be keeping both Iain's and Amy's families informed and trying to make their wait less harrowing. And she knew that he'd be giving all he had to make Amy's transplant operation a success.

But there was one moment for each other. One moment when she looked up into his eyes and saw the weight of responsibility. Saw the smile that told her he knew she was feeling it too. This wasn't just comfort for each other, it was the pathway that David had told her was so important. Creating joined-up care for patients and their families, helping them understand and see the right way forward.

Emma watched him go. Her appreciation of the way that Josh moved wasn't anywhere on David's list of things to do, but he'd told her that she would find her own ways of getting through the day. Whatever worked, worked.

A long day. A good day. Emma had taken advantage of a coffee break to slip into the viewing gallery to watch Josh operate. Amy's small form was all but obscured, but she easily picked Josh out from the shrouded figures around her, by the shooting stars cap. She smiled. He'd kept his promise to the little girl, even if she didn't have any way of knowing he had.

He'd been standing for three hours at that point, and would be doing so for at least another three, but he showed no sign of it. Josh was locked in deep concentration, seeming relaxed but totally focused. His back wouldn't ache, and he'd feel no hunger or fatigue until the operation was finished. Then it would all hit him.

She'd seen enough procedures to know that Josh ran his theatre well. He didn't have to look up to make sure that anyone was doing as he asked—Josh was in sole charge. As always, he had everything under control, right down to the last detail.

Ironic. That might be one of his worst failings when it came to a relationship, but it was a major asset in doing his job. Emma was too busy to address that thought at the moment…

But there was time later.

Once Josh had finished the operation, they had reported the good news on Amy's condition to her parents and left them with her in the recovery room. Josh looked tired now, the weariness of six hours' intense concentration finally catching up on him.

'You should go home.' She smiled up at him.

'You're not coming?' Weary as he was, the implications of her words didn't quite elude him.

'I want to speak with the donor and his family. And I've got a few other things to do, before I report back to David and tell him how it all went.'

And Emma wanted to take some time out to think. She'd been so wrapped up in her work today that the constant doubts about her relationship with Josh hadn't had time to surface. Now that they had, it was possible to look at them with fresh eyes, and that new perspective was making her wonder what on earth she thought she was doing. Sleeping with Josh, getting involved again, when there was no way forward with him.

'I'll leave the car if you're going to be coming home late.'

No. She didn't want that. She wanted to be cut adrift from Josh for a while, because being with him didn't allow her to think straight.

'Take it. I'll get a taxi if it's late.'

He nodded, shooting her that delicious smile that made all of her doubts disappear. Right now, Emma didn't want them to go anywhere because they were the one thing that were holding her down, grounding her. Without them she was rudderless, and liable to make mistakes.

'Okay. Shall I save you something to eat?'

'No thanks. I don't know how long I'll be

and… Don't wait up for me. I may catch a few hours' sleep here.'

The flicker at one side of his eye told her that he could feel her drawing away from him. Or maybe he was too tired to feel anything at the moment. Josh lifted his hand, brushing his fingers against her sleeve.

'I'll see you when I see you, then.'

Josh's back ached and he was hungry. He eased the knots from his shoulders as he waited in line at the cafeteria for coffee and a sandwich, and then walked to his car.

A good night's sleep in one of the on-call rooms generally required a greater level of fatigue than Emma was carrying around at the moment. He couldn't shrug off the nagging feeling that something wasn't right, but Emma didn't have to explain her decisions to him. Maybe he was just becoming hyper-sensitive, and that wouldn't do because he'd promised her a relationship without any strings.

Sleep wasn't difficult when he arrived home, and he woke up at three in the morning, still on the sofa. For a moment he felt the thrill of wondering whether he'd woken because Emma had arrived home, and then in the still darkness he realised she hadn't. When he went upstairs, hoping she might have gone to bed without waking him, the bedroom was dark and empty.

Josh flung himself down on the bed, staring up at the ceiling. He'd known that this would happen and he felt...just the familiar numbness of having to move on, because he'd done it too many times before and feeling loss would be too overwhelming. He should just accept it, because it went with the territory where Emma was concerned.

But he was wide awake, now. And without even thinking about it, he'd gone into the bathroom and splashed water on his face, dropped his clothes into the washing basket and pulled out a pair of old jeans and a sweater. He then spent ten minutes looking for his car keys, before going downstairs to the garage.

Josh had expected to have to hunt for Emma, but he saw her as he drove into the hospital, standing outside the main entrance with a man. He kept her in his rear-view mirrors as he drove along the slip road into the car park, and saw a taxi draw up in front of her. Maybe she *was* on her way home to him. But the thrill of the thought turned into dashed hopes as he saw the man get into the taxi, and it drew away, leaving Emma standing alone.

Now wasn't the time for dashed hopes. It wasn't the time for feeling nothing either. He got out of the car and walked across to the bench where she was sitting, the lights from the reception area glinting in her hair.

He sat down. Neither of them said a word for what seemed like an age.

'That was the donor's partner. I've only just managed to persuade him that sitting in the waiting room all night isn't going to help anyone.'

So she really did have something to do here tonight. Josh nodded, silently wondering if she'd reckoned on this when she'd told him that she wasn't coming home. That was probably an unfair question.

'What are you doing here, Josh?' Emma was staring straight ahead of her. 'We said—'

'Yeah, we did, didn't we? No strings. I get that, and I'm already forgetting what your face looks like.'

He could tell that had hurt her. Had he gone out to hurt her, just to see what it looked like and maybe to feel a little bit of it? Emma had turned away from him, now.

'How many friends do you have from before medical school? And when you were at medical school?'

Josh saw anger in her slight shrug. That was okay, not knowing how many meant there were some, and that was answer enough.

'Loads, I imagine. I'll bet you keep in touch and meet up from time to time. I don't have a single one. That was what I learned during my first ten years. That having to move on hurts. And I didn't want to feel that hurt. So I tried to switch it off. When my mother died, I just packed my rucksack and walked away, and I hated David for bringing me back and making me feel the loss.'

Emma turned, suddenly. 'What's this all about, Josh?'

'I'm guessing that you've been having your reservations about sleeping with me. Maybe today put everything into perspective.' He felt a lump rise in his throat. But this was what it was all about, wasn't it? Making yourself address the hard issues so that you didn't lose someone completely.

She heaved a sigh, and then her lips formed a reluctant smile. 'All right. Since you're going to be an adult about this, I'm not going to let you outdo me. Yes, today put things in perspective. And I am wondering what we think we're doing.'

'Me too. I know I'm losing you and...' Josh shrugged. This next part was the hardest thing to say. 'Forget the sex for a moment; what I really care about is keeping our friendship. Whatever you do and whatever you say, I'm not going to just let you drift away without putting up a fight. I'm not going to accept it and walk away.'

Emma raised her eyebrows. 'You want to forget the sex?'

'Okay. So it's unforgettable. But I have to, just for the moment, if I'm going to feel what losing your friendship is like. And learn to fight for it.'

'That's—' she gave him a sudden smile '—one of the nicest things anyone's ever said to me.'

'That they want to be your friend?' Josh reckoned that many, many people had said that to Emma in the course of her life, and that she'd had little difficulty in keeping her side of the bargain.

'That you'll fight for me.' She reached out and took his hand. 'I'll fight for you too.'

He nodded, wondering if Emma knew how much this meant to him. Whether she understood that what came so naturally to her was something he had to struggle with. Then he felt her fingers tightening hard around his.

'I'd really like to be your first, Josh.'

'My first?' At the moment he was feeling too much to fathom quite what she meant.

'The first friend that you don't let go of.'

'Ah. Yeah, I'd like that too.'

She leaned towards him, and he felt her shiver. Taking off his jacket, Josh wrapped it around her shoulders, holding it in place with a hug.

'What about the sex?'

Josh swallowed hard. Looked up at the sky that was beginning to show the first traces of light.

'I… It's not as important as… I don't want this to be all or nothing, Em.'

'I get that. Now that we've agreed that it's not going to be *nothing*... Do you have any difficulties with *all*?'

He felt her move against him and knew that she was looking up at him. Josh couldn't quite meet her gaze at the moment.

'If…um… I was thinking maybe you did, since you stayed here tonight.'

Emma moved again, whispering in his ear. She had the *all* part of their relationship down to a very fine art and Josh tried to calm the shivers that were running through him. Closing his eyes didn't help in the slightest.

'We both have to be back here again in five hours. And you haven't had any sleep.' He dared to look down at her, and her smile aroused him even more than her words.

'I had a nap in your office for a couple of hours. If you drag those two easy chairs together, they're actually very comfortable.' Emma stretched up to kiss his cheek. 'We could try rushing?'

There was nothing more to be said. Josh got to his feet and caught her hand, hurrying over towards his car.

CHAPTER THIRTEEN

THIS WAS MADNESS. Josh had been hurt enough already. She'd been hurt too, and Emma needed to find a place in her life that allowed her to move forward. She doubted very much if she could do that while she was with Josh. But that one word—doubt—held the key to everything. While there was still one chance that they might work things out, Emma couldn't leave him.

And it was working now. She'd taken fright and Josh had dismissed her fears and come to fetch her. He'd fought for her and that meant a lot.

Amy was making a good recovery, and left the Paediatric Intensive Care Unit on the third day after her operation. Iain too was recovering well. He was still in pain, but if anything, he felt more positive about his experience than he had before, saying that his gift was no longer just something he felt was right, but was now a part of who he was. Emma had suggested that he make a video diary, and had been in his room recording the first entry.

He'd finally said all that he wanted to say for today and started to doze. Emma walked back to Josh's office.

'Hey. How did it go?'

'Good. Donating part of his liver has been a life-changing experience, and however positive he feels about it, it's still good to talk and make sense of it.'

Josh nodded. 'It sounds like a worthwhile project. Something that the foundation might be interested in taking forward.'

'They do that kind of thing already, don't they?' Emma sat down in one of the visitors' chairs.

'They record interviews with donors and recipients, for the website. This isn't quite the same thing though; it's more a matter of a personal journey. Why don't you ask Dad?'

Emma nodded. 'I did mention that I was doing it. He said he'd be interested in hearing how it went.'

Josh chuckled. 'Sounds to me as if he's hooked, and he's just waiting to see what you come up with. He does that kind of thing. We could brainstorm, if you like?'

'Brainstorm. Josh, have you not got anything better to do? Something like surgery?'

'Actually, no. I had a surgery cancelled this afternoon. If you don't want to brainstorm, you could always let your hair down…'

'Don't tempt me, Josh. And might I just mention that most people who have worked late every night for the last week would be thanking their lucky stars for a couple of free hours and the prospect of going home on time.' It was just as well that Josh thrived on being busy, because he usually was.

He didn't get the chance to answer, because Emma's phone started to buzz and she took it out of her pocket, scanning the message that had popped up. 'I've got to go now, I'm wanted in A & E. So you'll have to find something else to keep you amused.'

'Someone's talked you into covering? Why didn't they ask me?'

'I offered. Whoever's on the rota for today is off sick.' Emma fiddled with the app. 'Is there some way I can confirm, and say I'm on my way?'

'Just hit "accept."' Josh was on his feet now too, and making for the door. 'This way. It's quicker.'

He led her down a deserted back staircase and into a service lift, then along a couple of corridors and across a small quadrangle, ending up at one of the side entrances to the hospital's A & E department, in about a quarter of the time that it would have taken Emma to get down to the main reception and then along to A & E. Josh made a beeline for a young doctor who seemed to be doing three things at once, and she shot him a smile.

'To what do we owe this honour, Mr Kennedy? Or have you just lost your way?'

Josh chuckled. 'I was actually making sure the doctor you requested made it down here without getting lost.' He made a quick introduction. 'Emma Owen... Demi Angelou.'

'Thanks for coming so quickly.' Demi turned to Emma, handing her a folder with a patient assessment form clipped to the front. 'I've got a forty-five-year-old male, with symptoms of moderate liver failure. I can get him an early appointment with a consultant, but I'd prefer someone took a look at him now.'

That was wise. Patients with liver failure often didn't experience drastic symptoms until the damage was too great to correct easily, but finding out exactly what was wrong took time and Emma could see that the A & E department were busy.

'Leave it with me. Have you asked for an ultrasound?'

'Yep, the nurse has already given him plenty of water to drink and they're sending a technician down. Might be a while though.'

Emma looked up at Josh, who was clearly trying to read the notes over her shoulder without being too obtrusive about it.

'Care to do the honours?' She smiled up at him.

'Yeah. Thanks.'

Demi snorted with laughter. 'I'm just going to pretend that we don't have a hotshot surgeon down here offering to do ultrasound scans. It might go to my head.' She looked up as someone beckoned to her. 'Unfortunately I can't hang around to watch. Cubicle Four...'

Terry Adams looked older than his forty-five years and was ashen and clearly in pain. Emma introduced herself and Josh, and the woman sitting by his bedside brightened immediately.

'Thank goodness. I don't think that young girl knew very much at all.'

'She's young but extremely talented.' Josh issued the reproach so pleasantly that it clearly didn't register as one, but the woman stopped complaining.

Emma sat down and started to go through Terry's medical history with him, referring to Demi's notes as she went. Terry's responses were limited mostly to nods, and it was his wife, Janet, who answered most of the questions.

She moved on to her examination, probing his stomach. 'Does that hurt?'

'He said it hurt a little further down,' Janet answered.

Emma ignored her, turning to Terry. 'I need you to tell me, Terry.'

'A bit...' Terry nodded.

'Right, then, it looks as if Mr Kennedy's ready with the ultrasound...' She glanced at Josh and he nodded. 'It won't hurt at all, but there's a cold sensation on your skin from the gel.'

Josh smiled at Terry, and started the examination, with just the same care and concentration that he took when he was in the operating theatre. Janet was watching him, leaning round to see the display, and that gave Emma the chance to talk to Terry.

'How many units of alcohol do you drink a week, Terry?'

'None. I don't drink.'

'Okay, that's good news when you have the kind of pain you're experiencing. And have you been taking any medications? Either prescribed by your doctor, or off the shelf?'

'I get headaches—'

Janet turned, interrupting him. 'Migraines. He's been getting a lot of them recently and he has to have something for them.'

'What do you take?' Emma doggedly continued to question Terry, and he gave her the name of the tablets he took. 'And you take them according to the instructions on the packet?'

'Of course he does.' Emma ignored Janet's reply and waited for Terry's.

'Sometimes I take a few more. It doesn't do any harm and when the headaches are bad...'

'All right. Well, as a general piece of advice, you mustn't ever take more than the recommended dose. I know it's sometimes tempting when you have a bad headache, but these are quite strong and it's easy to take too much when you're not feeling well.' Emma waited for Terry's nod before she continued. 'Anything else?'

'Just Janet's herbal pick-me-ups. I'd like to lose a bit of weight.'

'They won't do him any harm. It's just herbs.' As expected, Janet had something to say about it. Emma wondered whether she should mention foxgloves and digitalis to her, and decided against it. This was a stressful situation for her too, and it was probably just the way she was coping with it, however annoying it seemed.

'What's the name of the supplement you're using?'

Josh had obviously seen the direction that Emma was going in, and interjected with a few questions that she'd already asked. That diverted Janet's attention for long enough to allow Emma to pull out her phone and look up the herbal supplements to see what they contained.

He finished the ultrasound, replying to Janet's questions with a lot more patience than Emma could have mustered. She got to her feet, telling Terry that she'd be back in a moment, and holding the door open while Josh manoeuvred the ultrasound trolley outside.

'Did you find anything?' she asked after closing the door behind them.

'There's a slightly increased echogenicity, indicating steatosis, but it doesn't account for the symptoms.' Josh frowned. 'How about you?'

'Terry doesn't drink, but he does take painkillers for migraine pretty regularly. He admitted that on a couple of occasions he's taken a little more than the recommended dosage.'

Josh nodded. 'If he's owned up to it, then he might well be doing it on a regular basis. Did you find out what were in those herbal supplements?'

'Yes, and a couple of the ingredients are contraindicated for liver damage. I think we need to keep him in for a couple of days to do some more tests, but at the moment it looks as if we have a case of DILI on our hands.'

'I agree. You want me to go upstairs and arrange for a bed for Terry?'

'Don't pretend that you don't want to see things through. Just make the call up to the unit, the way you usually would. You can come and break the news with me.' Telling a patient that they may have a drug-induced liver injury, which they'd inadvertently caused themselves, always required a degree of tact.

'Right. Didn't want to crowd you.' Josh gave her a smouldering look, which Emma did her best to ignore.

He was positive and kind, telling Terry and Janet that he'd seen no signs of serious liver disease, although the slightly brighter patches on the ultrasound image did indicate that there were some fatty deposits in the liver.

'This kind of thing is typically picked up in just these circumstances, where we do some tests for another reason. It can often be improved significantly by diet and losing a little weight, so this is a good opportunity to do something about it before it becomes problematic.'

'So this isn't what's making me feel so rough.' Terry understood immediately and Josh nodded, glancing at Emma in an indication that this next part was for her to explain.

'My initial thoughts, Terry, are that the pain and nausea you're feeling right now is due to the medications you've been using. We'd like to admit you for a couple of days so that we can do some tests to confirm that.'

'What? But...' The expected objection came

from Janet, but her combative tone had disappeared. She was as white as a sheet, tears forming in her eyes.

Terry reached out and took her hand. 'Let's just listen to what the doctor has to say, eh, love?'

Janet looked as if she was about to faint, and Josh reached for a tissue, giving her an encouraging smile.

'This isn't uncommon.' It wasn't particularly common either, but Emma decided to emphasise the positive. 'And the good news is that the liver is amazing. It's a kind of detox centre for the rest of the body, and that means it's capable of filtering out waste products and even regenerating itself if necessary. We just have to allow it to do so, by finding out exactly what's causing the damage.'

'And you think…my migraine tablets?' Terry frowned.

'Most over-the-counter painkillers are very safe drugs to take, but it's really important that you don't exceed the recommended dose because taking too many of them can cause liver damage. I've taken a look at the herbal preparation you've been using, and that does contain a very high concentration of products that have been found to compromise liver function in some circumstances as well. As I said, we'll be doing some other tests to make sure that everything else is in good shape, but it's likely that all you need to do is discontinue the medication you've been taking, and give your liver a chance to recover.'

'But...the headaches.' Terry's brow creased. 'They get really bad sometimes.'

'Have you spoken with your own doctor about them?'

'No, I just... We got some tablets from the chemist and they seemed to be working.'

'Well, I think we might be able to make things better for you there as well. We can discuss some of the things that may be triggering your migraines and suggest some alternative medicines to control it.'

Janet's shoulders were drooping and she covered her face with her hands. 'It's all my fault.'

'That's not true, Mrs Adams,' Josh replied quickly. 'The very best thing you could have done was to bring your husband here to see Dr Owen today.'

'But the herbal remedies...' Janet wasn't about to let herself off the hook so easily.

'Were an honest mistake. Let's fix it now, shall we?' Emma added.

'Yes. Yes, we'll fix it, Terry.' Janet took her husband's hand.

It was seven o' clock before they got home. Josh had spent over an hour with Janet, reassuring her and talking to her about how the liver functioned and ways in which diet could improve the mild steatosis he'd seen, and Emma had been concentrating on Terry, and putting some of the tests she wanted into motion. By the time they left, Janet and Terry seemed like different people, relaxed and chatting to the nurses, and Janet was thanking them for all that they were doing.

'Dad calls it hospitalitis.' Josh grinned at her as he opened the front door of the mews house. 'People feel there's something wrong and they just hope it'll get better on its own. By the time they get to the hospital they're so stressed about everything that they actually don't hear a word that anyone's saying to them.'

'I'm glad that Terry didn't wait any longer. DILI is a very slippery slope.'

'Yeah. You probably saved him an encounter with me in the operating theatre.'

Emma laughed, rolling her eyes. 'That's the general plan, Josh. I'd be more than happy if I could halve your workload by educating people about how to look after themselves.'

'I'd spend the extra time listening to you talk about the liver. Did you know your eyes light up when you talk about how it regenerates?'

'Don't you think it's amazing?' Emma threw herself onto the sofa, tugging at her hair. Friend time, although the lines were becoming increasingly blurred between their various personas.

'Yeah, I do. Even more so when I hear you talk about it. Glass of wine?'

'Thanks. Just a half-glass.'

He poured two half-glasses of wine, picking up his tablet. Josh always checked his personal email as soon as he got home. Once a day was enough, and it usually took him a few minutes to tap out his replies, and then he put the tablet aside and left it alone.

But this time he was reading something carefully, hands planted on the countertop, head bowed in concentration. He reached for his glass, almost knocking over the other one, but didn't seem to notice. Maybe this was Jamie. Josh hadn't said a word about it, but Emma knew that he was hoping for an email from him.

Or maybe David had taken it into his head to write one of his long, bullet-pointed emails, and Josh would be tapping out a brief *yes, okay* in reply any minute now. Emma sat for a few minutes, while he finished reading, and then decided that the wait would be better with a glass in her hand.

When she walked across to the kitchen, picking up her wine, he didn't seem to even notice her. But as she turned to leave him he pushed the tablet towards her, his face impassive.

Jamie. Emma saw the name at the top. She picked up the tablet, walking slowly back to the sofa as she read, hoping that Josh might snap out of his reverie and follow her. She read carefully, and began to see why he hadn't.

The tone of Jamie's email was different from the first, with none of the excitement and warmth he'd displayed. This was in turns apologetic and formal, as Jamie explained that he'd told his father about his contact with Josh and he hadn't reacted well. If Jamie had anything to do with Josh he was on his own. There would be no more family, no funding for uni; he'd be cut off completely. Jamie had ended with a half-hearted suggestion that they might meet in secret, but it was clear that he didn't think that was a good idea.

'Josh, I'm so sorry.'

'It's okay.' He shrugged, emptying his glass in one gulp. 'I took a risk. There was always that possibility.'

He opened the fridge, refilling his glass again. It wasn't like Josh to drink a second glass of wine, but at least he put the bottle back again. In his shoes, Emma would probably have kept hold of it to save herself another journey.

'Do you have any idea what you're going to say to him?'

'Yeah.' He joined her on the sofa, his long legs sprawling out in front of him. 'I'd already thought about it and I'm going to write back and tell him it's okay. And that I'll always be here, and he can contact me whenever he wants.'

'That's generous of you.'

'What am I going to do, Em? He's twenty years old and the father he's known all his life is threatening to cut him off.'

'It might be just an empty threat.'

'You'd take that chance? He's done it before.'

Josh was right. This must be cutting him into little pieces, but he'd said nothing about what he wanted or needed, just tried to do the right thing by a brother he hadn't even met.

'You're right. I hope I'd be brave enough to do what you're doing and make sure that Jamie's okay.'

He put his glass down. 'Will you just…come here?'

It was easy to slide across and hug him, and Josh held her tight. Less easy to wonder whether she wasn't doing just the same as Jamie had just done. Offering Josh something, in the knowledge that she'd be leaving soon. Saying that they'd promised each other nothing was a cop-out, because their unspoken promises had been made every night, in his bed.

'What I really want to do is make a visit to my biological father. Maybe punch him around a bit and tell him that he has no right to tell me what I can and can't do. Or Jamie, for that matter; he's an adult. And that if he doesn't step up to his responsibilities towards him, then he'll be hearing from me again.'

Emma squeezed him tight. 'And you're a surgeon. You know just where to punch.'

'Yes, I do.'

Now wasn't the time to talk about her own doubts, or her growing guilt. Josh needed her tonight. 'What do you say we go out for dinner? I know a great place in South Kensington; it's my treat. We'll walk there to clear out the cobwebs.'

'I'm getting dinner, am I? I'll have to make you feel sorry for me a little more often.'

'I don't feel sorry for you, Josh. I'm proud of you.'

'That's a bit harder to earn. In that case, I'll accept your offer.'

She'd never known Josh to ask for any sympathy over anything. He didn't waver, whatever happened, and that was one of the things that made him a good surgeon. Decisive, cool and in control. However much he was hurting.

'I'm going to go and get changed, then. Are you coming?'

'In a minute. I'm going to write back to Jamie.'

'Now?' Maybe that was overdoing the decisiveness.

'That must have been a difficult email for him

to write—he could have just not written back. I want him to know that I appreciate his honesty and that keeping his family is the right thing to do. And I want to be a friend to him, even though he can't be a friend back.'

Emma kissed him. 'You're not going to let him go?' Every time she started to wonder what she was doing with Josh, he did something that gave her hope.

'No. I want him to know that whatever he does, I'll be there for him. I've learned that from some important people in my life.'

David. His mother. Maybe a little part of it from her, but Emma wasn't sure that she deserved any credit for it. She was just holding on, closing her eyes and hoping that somehow this would all work out.

'Write your email.' She wriggled out of his embrace and stood up. 'I'm going to find something really nice to wear tonight.' Josh always took notice of what she wore and Emma liked his appreciative glances.

'Do *not* tempt me to come up there with you and devise a strategy on getting you back out of the really nice thing as soon as you've got into it.'

'I expressly forbid it, Josh. I prefer your talent for spontaneity when you're engaged in getting me out of my clothes.'

She heard him chuckle behind her as she climbed the stairs.

* * *

It was one of the hardest emails he'd ever had to write, and if he allowed himself to think about it too much he'd lose his nerve. But Emma made it easier, walking back downstairs in a wraparound top that hugged her figure and looked as if it might take a little strategising before he could work out exactly how it was fastened. Casual trousers and flat shoes showed that she was serious when she'd said they'd walk.

She sat down, reading the email he'd written carefully. Finally she nodded. 'That's perfect, Josh. It doesn't leave any room for doubt, but you've also made it clear that you'll welcome any contact from him in the future if things change.'

'Right.' His courage failed him. 'Will you send it, then?'

'You're sure?'

'I'm sure. Send it.'

He heard the tone as the email was sent. Then Emma powered the tablet down, and clipped the cover in place, tucking it away in the bookcase. 'Go and get changed. Hurry up, I'm already hungry.'

She was always a delight, but tonight Josh was realising the full meaning of that. It wasn't something fragile, which might fail at any time; her charm had muscle behind it. He needed to walk tonight, to laugh and feel the evening breeze on his face. He needed Emma, and she didn't fail him.

* * *

He'd been doubtful that he'd be able to eat too much, but by the time they reached the restaurant he was hungry. Emma had chosen a place that served simple food that was fresh and flavourful, and although she thought the chocolate pudding a little too sweet when she leant over to taste his, Josh reckoned it was just right.

His phone buzzed and he automatically picked it up, without thinking that he'd decided not to look at his email again tonight. When he saw the notification, he couldn't put it back down again.

'It's an email. From Jamie.'

Emma's expression became suddenly thoughtful. 'I guess… You know it's there now, Josh. You're only going to be wondering what it says, all the way home.'

The email was just one line and Josh handed Emma the phone so that she could read it too.

'That's nice. Do you suppose he knows that *au revoir* really means *I'll see you later*?'

'I don't know.' But Jamie had thanked him and called him brother. That on its own meant a lot.

She closed the email, laying the phone back down on the table. 'This tells me that he understands, Josh. Whatever happens next, I hope you'll always feel that you handled this compassionately and thoughtfully. Because that's what I see.'

'It hurts.' Two little words that were so difficult to say.

'I see that too. Would you like to go?'

Josh shook his head. He'd lost Jamie, at least for a while. But Emma was still here and she'd given him the strength to go through with what he felt was right.

'Shall we have coffee?' He pushed the rest of the chocolate pudding aside.

They lingered over coffee, Emma clearly making an effort to lift his mood. And then suddenly he stopped noticing that, because the constriction in his chest had eased and he felt able to smile again.

Josh insisted that he hail a taxi for the journey home, reckoning that she'd walked far enough already and she must be tired. But Emma leaned forward, stopping the taxi and getting out when they were half a mile from home. The cool, evening air cleared his head and he followed Emma up the stairs, pulling her close to kiss her. He wanted her more than ever.

'I think I've worked out my strategy on your top.'

Her eyes were bright and clear tonight, seeming to see right into him. 'You may find that my ingenuity slows you down a bit.'

'My strategy will trounce your ingenuity.'

'You reckon so?'

She broke away from him, running up the second flight of stairs. Josh caught her at the top, kissing her again; turning her towards the bedroom door in a slow dance. One day he might hear from Jamie again. But in the meantime, his family were the people he chose, and the woman he chose was in his arms.

CHAPTER FOURTEEN

JOSH SEEMED A little thoughtful as they walked to
the hospital the next morning, but his ready smile
seemed to indicate that the thoughts weren't bad
ones. Maybe he'd been expecting something like
this, and his biological father's second rejection
came as no great surprise. Or maybe he was in
denial; it was sometimes difficult to tell.

He was in the operating theatre this morning,
which always seemed to subsume any of his other
emotions for a while. Emma had a long list of
things to do, as well as liaising with David over
another patient whose transplant he'd been supervising, so she'd been busy as well.

At lunchtime she ended the video call with
David, whose infectious smile stayed with her
all the way to Amy's bedside. The little girl was
yet another reason to smile. The yellowish tint of
her skin and sclera was much less pronounced,
and there were no signs that her body was re-
jecting the new liver. Careful pain management
meant that she was comfortable and responsive,

and Julie seemed less exhausted as well. Emma spent some time with them, answering Julie's questions and listening to Amy's plans for what she was going to do when she was well.

Then she saw Iain.

He seemed rather more subdued today, maybe as a result of his pain meds having been reduced, and when Emma asked how he was feeling Peter answered.

'He hasn't eaten any lunch.'

In Emma's experience visitors and family could often provide valuable information. They saw the small changes in someone that were often missed by busy medical staff.

'Okay. Iain, are you in pain?'

'It's not so bad. I've just had half my liver removed, remember.' Iain gave her a wan smile.

And sometimes patients were the last people you should ask. Iain was clearly in pain, and when Emma pulled on a pair of gloves and checked his stomach, it was a little bloated. His blood pressure and pulse were normal, but his temperature was a little high.

'How long have you been feeling like this, Iain?'

'My stomach's not been so good since I woke up this morning. It's probably from too much time in bed. Although…uh… I feel sick.'

Emma managed to catch up one of the disposable vomit bowls from beside the bed, as Iain began to retch. She signalled to Peter to press the call button to summon a nurse, and Iain sank back onto the pillows. He was clutching his stomach now, clearly in a lot of discomfort.

A nurse arrived, and Emma slipped out of the room for a moment. Both Iain and Peter had read every piece of available information on liver transplants and she didn't want them jumping to any conclusions until she'd discussed her provisional diagnosis. She dialled the number for the Transplant Unit's reception.

'It's Emma Owen—is Alex Sargent available, please?'

'No, he's in surgery. Can anyone else help?'

This couldn't wait. 'Josh Kennedy, then.'

'Yes, he's here. Putting you through.'

The sound of retching came from Iain's room again and Emma turned to look through the open door. The nurse was dealing with it, but it was looking increasingly likely that Iain was going to need at least a diagnostic procedure.

'Emma?' Josh asked, sounding concerned.

'Josh, are you available to come and see Iain Warner, Amy's donor? Alex is in surgery and I suspect a biliary leak. We're in Room 407.' Emma wasn't going wait for Alex to be available just because Josh had been Amy's surgeon. There was no question of any conflict of interest now, in getting Iain the best treatment as soon as she possibly could.

'Sure. I'll be right up.' Josh ended the call abruptly.

By the time he arrived, Iain was lying back down again. The nurse had a fresh vomit bowl ready, in case it should be needed, and Peter was sitting by the bed holding Iain's hand. Every head in the room swivelled towards Josh, as he picked up the notes at the end of the bed.

'Hi, Iain, I'm Josh Kennedy and I'm a consultant transplant surgeon.'

'You're not the right guy.'

Josh looked up from the notes and chuckled. 'Yeah, story of my life. Mr Sargent's not available at the moment and so I'm going to take a look at you if I may.'

'Yes…' Iain winced again, from another wave of pain.

'First things first. Let me take a look at your incision.'

'Sure. If you can find it. I'm personally rather disappointed…' Iain attempted a joke.

'I wouldn't get your hopes up, Iain. Mr Kennedy doesn't give his patients scimitar-shaped scars just for show either.' Emma grinned back at Iain, and Peter suddenly snorted with laughter. The tension in the room broke, and Peter allowed

Emma to lead him away from Iain's bedside and guide him firmly towards the doorway.

'I need you to wait outside for a moment, Peter. We'll call you when we're finished.'

Peter had stopped laughing now. 'What's the matter with him, Emma?'

'That's what we're trying to find out. Let us take care of him.'

'Okay.' Peter turned suddenly, leaving the room.

Josh's examination was quick, but his jokes and relaxed style were enough to put Iain at ease. Every patient was different, and a doctor didn't always have the time to assess which atmosphere would put them most at ease. But the trust that had grown between Emma and Josh allowed her to shortcut the process for him. It also allowed Josh to assess Iain's responsiveness and his level of pain better. Emma watched as he discounted each possibility in turn, leaving only one conclusion.

'I think you're right.' He murmured the words to her, as he turned to fetch Peter back to sit with Iain.

'Iain, your symptoms suggest that you have a biliary leak. It's not uncommon after liver surgery, and as this has been caught early we can rectify it very easily.'

'He could have said something sooner.' Peter

gave Iain a reproachful look, which Iain ignored completely.

'Now is soon enough.' Josh gave Peter a reassuring smile and turned back to speak to Iain. 'I'd like to do an ERCP, which involves passing a very small tube from your mouth to your stomach, so we can see what's going on. I'll have the anaesthetist come and see you to discuss the options, but usually this procedure is done under sedation. Depending on the exact nature of the problem I may also be able to rectify it without the need for surgery.'

Iain glanced at Peter and then nodded. 'Yeah. That sounds good, thanks.'

'I'll prescribe something for the pain in the meantime, and get someone to sort out the consent forms, while I check on theatre availability. Have you had lunch?'

'Couldn't face it.'

'When was the last time you ate or drank anything?'

'Breakfast. I've had some sips of water since.'

'Okay, don't have anything to eat or drink for the time being.' He glanced at the nurse, who nodded.

'Thank you, Doctor.' Peter spoke up. 'What does ERCP stand for?'

Josh grinned. 'Endoscopic retrograde cholangiopancreatography.' He could see where the question was going as well as Emma could, and clearly Peter was going to have difficulty typing that into a search engine. 'I think Dr Owen's probably your best bet if you have any questions.'

It was two hours before Josh could secure a slot in the endoscopy department for Iain, which wasn't a bad thing because it meant that Iain would have been fasting for eight hours, and there was no need to take the precaution of a general anaesthetic with rapid sequence induction. At St Agnes, Emma's home hospital in Liverpool, ERCPs were usually done by gastroenterologists, but Josh was qualified to perform the procedure. His ongoing care of his transplant patients made this a valuable addition to his skills.

His professional demeanour when he asked Emma if she'd be joining him pleased her, but she reminded herself she'd be involved with Iain's care when he returned to Liverpool, so it was a matter of continuity, rather than any personal consideration.

Emma gave Iain a little wave as he was wheeled into the theatre, just so that he'd know it was her behind the mask. Josh's headspace was already in surgical mode, watchful and concentrated. The nurse helped Iain up onto the couch, getting him to lie on his side, and he smiled nervously at Emma.

'When do I get the happy stuff?'

'You're getting it now.' The anaesthetist was already administering the sedative via a catheter that had been attached to the back of Iain's hand. It was fast-acting, and Iain would be starting to doze soon.

'You're gonna need all this?' Iain's speech was already beginning to slur slightly and he was looking around at the screens and other technology that surrounded him.

'Only the best for our donors.' Josh's voice sounded behind her. 'X-ray equipment here, and there's the display for that. This screen's for the camera, mounted on the probe...'

Iain had been trying to follow what Josh was saying, but his eyelids were drooping. When they closed, Josh glanced at the anaesthetist, who nodded back at him. They were ready to start.

Josh fitted a mouth guard and then began to pass the endoscope into Iain's mouth and down into his stomach. It was careful, concentrated work, watching the screen, which relayed the images from the camera, to make sure that he did no damage. When the camera reached the bile duct, a fine tube was passed down the endoscope and dye injected. The radiographer operated the X-ray equipment, and an image flashed onto the screen that was adjusted to Josh's eye level.

'Ah. There see, there's a leak in one of the

ducts on the cut surface of the liver.' Josh indicated the area on the screen, and Emma heard the click of the camera as he saved an image. He'd been documenting the whole process carefully and that would form part of the notes she took back to Liverpool with her.

He inspected the cut surface of the liver carefully along with the surgical sutures. It was a painstaking process, but Emma knew that this must be done well to avoid the need for further procedures. Her back began to ache from standing in the same position, and the heavy protective apron she wore to shield her from the X-rays was becoming more burdensome by the minute, but Josh showed no signs of discomfort, completely focused on what he was doing.

Finally, he carefully withdrew the endoscope and Iain was readied to leave. He'd be taken to the recovery room first and then back to his room on the ward.

Josh stripped off his gloves and held the door open for her, the momentary twitch of his lips saying that he was allowing himself just one moment of chivalry, now that the serious business of the evening was done.

'I'll go and see Peter.' He pulled his apron off, finally allowing himself to stretch his shoulders. 'Just to let him know that Iain's okay and he should continue to make a good recovery.'

'I'll walk with you.' Emma smiled up at him, falling into step as he made his way to the relatives' waiting room.

Respect and friendship. It allowed them to work together well and that brought a depth and breadth to their relationship that they hadn't experienced the first time. They'd be going home soon, and when they got there he'd pull the fastenings from her hair. Then it would turn into something delicious.

Happy. That was a good word. So were laughter and caring. Loved and in love—those words had always been a little more problematic for Josh, but he was getting his head around them. He was sure that he'd said something of the sort to Emma last night.

There was only one problem. Iain was getting better by the day, and soon he'd be out of hospital and convalescing for a few days with his parents before going back up to Liverpool with Peter. Amy would be staying in hospital a little longer, but she'd improved so much that it was hardly possible to recognise the little girl he'd got to know. He'd given her the shooting stars cap, and she'd taken to wearing it whenever the doctors visited her bedside. That was all good, but the difficulty lay in the fact that Emma would be leaving too.

He had a plan though. Josh had been turning it over in his mind for days and it all fitted together perfectly. It had to be today, because Emma would be taking the train back to Liverpool first thing tomorrow, and it started with apricot jam and cappuccino because that was Emma's favourite Saturday morning breakfast in bed.

'You are too perfect.' She kissed him before getting out of bed. 'I think you might be a figment of my imagination.'

'How do I function when you're not around, then?'

She grinned. 'How do I know that you do? I might just have made up a whole load of things that you did when I wasn't around, like you do in dreams. Or perhaps it's all momentum. Like a stone rolling down a hill.'

Emma was teasing, but she might have inadvertently hit on something there. Josh was beginning to feel that whatever he did when she wasn't around *was* just a matter of momentum, carrying him forward to the time he'd see her again.

'I could ask you the same question.' He could, but Josh didn't reckon he had the imagination to conjure Emma up all by himself. She was too vivid, far too complex and entrancing.

'You've got a point.' She was heading for the shower, and Josh collected the plates together to take them downstairs. 'I'll have to do something really unexpected, that you couldn't possibly have dreamed up, and then you'll know you didn't make me up.'

She did those things all the time. And Josh was about to break all the rules too and do something unexpected…something that had a future. Something real.

It was a sunny day, and they strolled down to Portobello Market together. They considered the pros and cons of things they knew they weren't going to buy, had coffee and then did some more window-shopping.

'I've been meaning to ask you…' He'd been working his way around to this since they started to walk home, and seeming to get no closer to it. It was time to just say it.

'Yes?'

Josh took a breath. 'Would it be okay if I came up to Liverpool sometime, to see you?'

She thought for a moment. More than one moment—the pounding of his heart told him that.

'Yes. I'd really like that, Josh.' She smiled up at him. 'What we have…'

'I don't want to let it go either.' He could breathe again, and the other things he wanted to ask seemed so much easier. 'Next weekend?'

'Maybe the weekend after. I'll be busy when I get back and it'll give me two whole weeks to look forward to it.' She put her arm around his waist, pulling him closer as they walked.

Her agreement buoyed him and he could see his goal now, so he took his shot. 'We've needed another hepatologist on the unit for a while now. I made enquiries and they're looking to recruit someone but people with the right experience are hard to find. I'm sure Dad would give you a glowing reference and there'd be no problem over getting somewhere to live. I might have to get a smaller car, so that your Mini would fit into the garage...'

Suddenly the world turned again and everything he thought he'd gained was snatched away. Because Emma was staring up at him, a look of horror on her face.

Emma was glad that Josh had asked about visiting, because she'd been wondering how she might ask him up to Liverpool for the weekend. It seemed that they were both of the same mind, that their relationship was worth throwing the rulebook out of the window and just seeing where that went.

And then... Strip away the veneer of change and he was still the same Josh. Still aching for security and needing commitment. And she was still the Emma who needed to move on with her life, after her father's death. Keeping her wheels turning wasn't just about moving from place to place, it was about healing.

Maybe she could still do this. But *maybe* wasn't enough, and she shouldn't make promises that she didn't know she could keep.

'You mean…' She cleared her throat, trying to think straight. 'You think that I should move. Give up my job…?'

'Or I could move to Liverpool.'

Right. Now he was just clutching at straws. Josh was needed here, and that didn't make any sense at all.

'Josh, I'm sorry, but… I don't think that's a good idea. Not just yet.'

He fished his keys out of his pocket, opening his front door. Maybe that was an end to it, but his face was grave and the bright, sunshiny prospect of seeing him again in two weeks had suddenly tarnished as well.

She walked up the stairs, looking around the living area desolately. Suddenly, sitting down on Josh's sofa, or going to Josh's fridge to get some juice, was the kind of thing it was necessary to think about—not something you'd do naturally because you felt at home in his home.

'Em, don't you see it?' Clearly he wasn't going to let this go. 'Don't you feel that we should be together?'

'What I feel is that we've spent three weeks

together. It's been great—better than great—it's been wonderful. What we decided…that we'd just kiss goodbye and then let fate decide whether we bump into each other again…that's not what either of us wants now. But don't you think it's a bit early to start making the kind of commitment that means I give up my job and move down to London?'

He frowned. 'I'm not asking you to do all of the legwork, Emma. I said that I'd move…'

'No. That's not my point, Josh. My point is that *neither* of us should be moving, because…' They were both too fragile. Still looking for different things.

'Because what?' His face was stony. 'The least you could do is give me a reason.'

One that didn't make him feel that she was flinging everything he'd told her back in his face. Which was hard, because everything he'd told her had only brought her to the conclusion that they couldn't be together.

'We're very different people, Josh. You want commitment, and I… I can't give you that right now. I need to find a way of moving forward that means something to me, because…because I lost that when we were together the last time. And I can't lose it again, not now.'

Too much truth. Too much *painful* truth, which

had sounded through her words. His face darkened suddenly.

'You're saying that *I* took that away from you?'

'I'm saying that I lost it. Because I loved you and I shouldn't have.'

'No, Em. You should have loved me because I loved you. Because if we do love each other, then we can compromise.'

'I should go.' Emma couldn't risk their hearts breaking the way they had before. Maybe that was what love and honesty were. She'd always felt that Josh was the one who was risk-averse, but maybe it had been her all along. Loving him had shown her that she was afraid too, when she'd thought herself fearless.

He turned suddenly, an expression of rage on his face. 'No, Emma, I'm not going to watch you go. Not again.'

'What, you're going to lock me in?' She regretted the words as soon as they were said. Josh could no more do that than fly. 'Let's not do this, Josh. I refuse to say all the things I said before.'

Too late. They might remain unsaid but they both knew what she'd said and what he'd said. The words were still stuck in their heads.

'I said I wouldn't watch you go.' His tone was as cold as ice. 'I'm not trying to tell you what to do, I'm just saying what *I* can and can't do.'

He turned, walking back down the stairs,

his footsteps loud in the sudden silence. Emma called after him, but he didn't turn. She heard the sound of the garage doors, and when she ran to the kitchen window he'd backed the car out and was slamming the doors shut.

'Don't drive, Josh...' She leaned across the sink, reaching for the catch on the kitchen window. But he was already back in the car, driving slowly and carefully across the smooth cobblestones.

That was Josh all over. She would have slammed the Mini into first gear, stalled the engine a couple of times and then roared up the mews, preferably leaving a trail of exhaust fumes behind her. Josh wasn't like that. She'd seen it in the operating theatre with her own eyes. Stress just made him even more focused on the task in hand.

And there was no going back now. They'd taken a risk, knowing that things hadn't worked out between them the last time, thinking that they could shorten the odds with a few rules. Now it seemed an insane thing to do, but Emma was hurting enough already to know why they'd done it.

She couldn't think about that now. It was done and the past couldn't be changed. The future could, and hers lay in leaving before Josh came back and they argued again, maybe even more hurtfully, although it was difficult to see how anything could hurt much more than this.

She needed to go back to Liverpool and let him get on with his life. Maybe meet someone else...

Okay. Turned out there was something that could hurt more: the thought of Josh giving everything he'd given her to someone else. Emma walked upstairs and began to pack her bags.

CHAPTER FIFTEEN

JOSH HAD DRIVEN a long way. He'd crossed from Buckinghamshire into Oxfordshire before he realised which way he was going and turned back again. He knew that David would welcome him, and that whenever he wanted to talk he'd be there. Josh didn't want to talk right now though.

It was dark by the time he got back home. The faint hope that the lights would be on in his apartment hadn't been worth his time. When he walked upstairs, the living space was neat and quiet. Emma had done just as he'd asked her to, and hadn't made him watch her go.

He flopped down onto the sofa, staring at the ceiling. It would be two nights and a day before he got any relief from this feeling. The operating theatre was the one place in the world that blotted everything else out, because of Josh's intense concentration on the life that he held in his hands.

As to the rest of it… He loved Emma more than he'd thought he could ever love anyone. But he'd ruined her life as well, because she couldn't see a way forward with him. So she'd kept her wheels turning, because that was how she dealt with things. She was gone and somehow he had to find a way to make his life mean something again.

Emma had tried. She'd *really* tried. For the last two weeks, she'd spent twelve hours a day at work, and then gone home and spent her time cleaning. Last weekend she'd got to the point where her patients were clearly wondering when she'd leave them in peace, and her house couldn't take any more disinfectant. So she'd spent the whole weekend in bed.

None of it did a thing to lessen the pain or take her mind off things. This weekend she'd tried feeding ducks in the park, visiting an art gallery and going to the cinema. But however much she did, it all felt like spinning her wheels in cloying mud, leaving her stuck, motionless and unable to move forward. And no amount of listless misery and crying could get Josh out of her system.

If he hadn't cared, then that would have been some kind of closure. But Emma knew that he did. She knew that she'd hurt him but that he would forgive her in the blink of an eye. That was the problem—she'd go back to him and then hurt him again.

There were two solutions. She could tell herself that this would pass and keep on going. Past experience told her that it wasn't so easy to forget Josh, and this time there was so much more to forget. Or she could do something about it. But what? She couldn't go back but she couldn't go forward without Josh either.

It was time to make a gesture, one that forced them both to change. Something that could tap into the trust they'd built, as friends and colleagues, and allow them to work through their emotional differences. And in a sudden flash of inspiration, Emma knew just the thing...

Josh had been working every shift that came available. It was tiring, but it meant he slept at night, and didn't spend his days thinking too much about Emma.

He'd turned down an invitation from David and Val to spend this weekend with them in Oxfordshire. He'd go next weekend instead, and hope that Val didn't talk too much about Emma, because even if she missed his reaction to the mention of her name, he doubted that his father would. He heard the letterbox open and then snap shut again downstairs. Perhaps whatever the postman had for him this morning would take up a few minutes of his time, in a weekend that already seemed interminably long.

He walked downstairs and gathered the mail,

sorting through the letters. Bills, an invitation to a barbecue, a couple of medical journals... And a postcard. He flipped it over, wondering what on earth Gran was doing in Liverpool.

Emma. Just her name, nothing else. He shook his head. Didn't she know that postcards weren't just postcards? That they had a value far beyond a piece of card with a stamp on it? He flung the bundle of post back down onto the floor, and walked back upstairs, fuming.

Then it hit him. Emma knew exactly what a postcard meant to him: it was his gran's way of telling him that she'd never let him go. It was the message he'd wanted to send to her, and the one he'd yearned to receive from her. It was audacious, and full of Emma's ability to make the best of things.

He almost fell down the stairs in his haste. Sitting down at the foot of the stair, he picked up the postcard and studied it carefully. Nothing but her name, no clues that he could see in the picture. No kisses. He would have liked kisses—Emma had a thing or two to learn from Gran about postcard writing—but this was the most precious thing...

He knew now what Emma was saying to him. They might have nothing more to say to each other, they might have a sum total of nothing.

But she wouldn't give him up. She couldn't stop loving him.

He should phone her. Tell her that he'd find a way… Josh ran back up the stairs and grabbed his phone. But before he dialled, the elegance of Emma's gesture stopped him. They didn't have to rush to find answers, or agonise day and night about them. Emma was standing her ground, and she'd be waiting for him.

He picked up his jacket and keys, walking out of the mews apartment with a spring in his step for the first time in weeks. Josh had a postcard to buy, and he wanted to get a really nice one.

The weekend had been torture. Would Josh understand? Would he hear what she had to say to him, and would he even want it? When Emma arrived home on Monday evening, a postcard was lying behind the front door. She dropped her bags, picking it up.

The Tower of London. It was a nice picture. She hardly dared turn the postcard over, but she couldn't just stand here all night, looking at the image. She took a deep breath…

I'll wait for you, Emma.
Knowing you're there is everything. Always,
Josh

Emma sank to her knees, shaking with emotion. It was just one step, and there would have to be a second and then so many more. But they'd made it.

She went out at lunchtime the next day, bought another postcard and sent it. When she got home there was one from Josh, waiting for her. Each day she sent a postcard and each day there was one in return. She was beginning to dread Sunday, when there would be no post. A whole two days without the one thing that gave her hope, and something to look forward to. On Saturday, there was a postcard from the London Eye and she smiled as she bent to pick it up. Josh was clearly doing the same as she was, going further afield each day to find postcards to send.

I didn't get anything from you today.
But I'll always love you and trust that you're
there.
Josh

Dammit! She'd sent one and it had probably been delayed in the post. But Josh had trusted her enough to know that. The trust they'd built as colleagues and as friends was finally, finally seeping through into their emotional lives. And that was the sweetest thing imaginable.

* * *

Fourteen postcards. They were carefully tacked up on the wall, in order, so that Josh could read Emma's side of their daily conversation. It had started with just one word, and it was the word he loved the most in this world. Emma. Now the postcards were loving messages, which turned his whole world upside down. They were constant reminders that Emma was there for him, and if a postcard didn't arrive one day, he just looked forward to two the next morning.

If anyone had asked him, he would have said that this would be torture, a kind of punishment for them both for having dared to love each other. But it wasn't. They were learning to trust each other, to be together without the pressures that life had put on them both. It was a slow process, but it felt to Josh that it was going at just the right speed.

He spent Saturday morning at the hospital, going through patient notes and planning his schedule for the next week. It was no longer necessary to stay until fatigue forced him home again, and he walked back to Notting Hill after lunch, stopping to buy a window box and some plants. Many of the apartments in the mews had bright window boxes, and he'd never had the time to add to the display. But time was on *his* side, now.

He turned into the mews, and saw a car parked across the doors of his garage. And then he dropped his purchases and ran, because the car was a red Mini, and Emma was leaning up against its front wing, looking as if she'd just driven here straight from the sixties, in a pair of flared jeans, a rainbow-coloured top and the baker boy cap that suited her so well.

'You came.' Now that he could hold her, he could stop shaking.

'I couldn't help myself.' She reached up, laying her hand on his cheek. 'Are you ready for this, Josh?'

'I'm not sure I'll ever be truly ready for you, Em, that's one of the reasons I love you so much. But I do know one thing. I'll never give up on you. If I want to trust you, then I have to trust myself, and I've made that step now.'

He kissed her and she melted into his arms. 'I love you so much, Josh. I have all the future I need, right here with you. And I'm never giving up on you either.'

'I know. I knew it right from the first postcard. How long have you been waiting?'

'I've waited all my life to come home to you, Josh.'

He chuckled. 'You *are* my home. But I meant how long have you been waiting out here for me?'

'Half an hour. I was going to phone you, but

I'm glad I didn't. The look on your face when you saw me and dropped your shopping...' She grinned at him. 'What on earth is it anyway?'

'Nothing... Window boxes.' Josh kissed her again, feeling the warm excitement of her response. *This* was love. He knew it as surely as he knew himself.

'Window boxes? So pretty...' She kissed him back and suddenly window boxes became an object of intense interest to Josh.

'I'll go and fetch them.'

'One more kiss before you do. I love you, Josh.'

EPILOGUE

One year later

IT WAS THE kind of summer's day that was perfect for driving. They'd followed the 'Routes Bis,' taking their time in working their way across France via shady country roads and small villages, in a silver Lotus Elan. Tomorrow they'd arrive in the Côte d'Azur, where they could enjoy a luxurious week in Cerise's apartment, while she was on tour in Germany.

'Josh! Stop the car…'

He slowed, stopping in a lay-by. 'We've gone the wrong way again?'

The map slipped off her lap and into the footwell. 'No, I don't think so. I just really wanted to kiss you.'

'So it's a *real* emergency, then.'

He leaned over, taking her in his arms and kissing her. As urgently as anyone could wish.

'Six days… This marriage is going really well so far.'

Josh laughed. 'I can't see any way it could have been better.'

They'd been married in the tiny village church, close to where David and Val lived in Oxfordshire, and the reception had been held on the vast lawns of the manor house. The day had been perfect, full of sunshine and laughter and a lot of love.

Love had made everything fall into place. The weekends together, in Liverpool and London, when they'd talked all day and made love all night. The job offer that had allowed Emma the freedom to come home to Josh and London full-time. David had slowed down, cutting his frenetic work schedule in half to spend time with Val, and had offered Emma the job of her dreams, working at different hospitals around London with the GDK Foundation. The engagement ring that Josh had gone down on one knee to offer her, knowing that she'd accept. Two diamonds, separate but bound together in a tracery of gold.

It hadn't always been easy, but they'd held each other close, talking a lot and listening a lot. Slowly their life together had turned into something more beautiful than Emma could ever have imagined.

'You're my one, true home, Emma Kennedy.' Josh echoed the wedding vows they'd made to each other.

'And you're mine.' Emma leaned over so she could whisper in his ear. 'I've got a secret...'

'Already? You're keeping secrets from me?'

'Only for three hours. I was going to tell you tonight, but I can't wait.'

Josh laughed. 'Not being able to keep a secret is one of the things I love about you. So... Three hours ago we were still at the boarding house. We had breakfast...'

'Before breakfast.' Emma was almost dancing in her seat and Josh was looking increasingly mystified.

'Before that...you were in the bathroom. You screamed, I nearly jumped out of my skin and you shouted through the door that you'd just found the biggest spider you'd ever seen.'

'Josh! Since when have I been afraid of spiders? I was rather hoping you'd see through that excuse and barge in and demand to know what was going on.'

He stared at her. She could see the light beginning to dawn in his blue eyes. Emma reached down to her handbag and took out the pregnancy test, handing it to him.

'This...this is positive, right?'

'Yes, those lines mean positive. And I did three of them so—'

Josh let out a whoop that echoed across the

cornfields and sent birds flapping upwards from the trees by the side of the road.

'Three's a definite.' He was hugging her so tight now that she could hardly breathe. 'Are you all right? What made you do the test?'

'I'm fine. I was a bit late, but I thought that was because of the running around for the wedding. But then I just… I don't know how I knew but I did. I didn't tell you because I didn't want to disappoint you if it was just my imagination, but I bought the tests while I was in the pharmacy yesterday.'

'Emma.' He drew back, his hands on her shoulders. 'I'm not going to mollycoddle you. I'll send you out to the corner shop in the rain, and make you repair the car…'

'Really? I was hoping for breakfast in bed and back rubs.'

He grinned. 'You were?'

'Yes, because you do both of those very well and it would be a shame if I had to miss out. I've got a husband who'll love and protect me always. Our baby's going to need that as much as I do.'

He lay his hand on her stomach, tears in his eyes. 'I promise, little one. Always.'

This was real now. Emma flung herself towards him, wrapping her arms around his neck, joy bursting from her.

She felt Josh tapping urgently on her shoulder.

'Em… Em, loosen up a bit. You're strangling me.'

'Oh! Sorry.'

'That's okay. You want to go for a walk? I don't think I can sit still enough to drive at the moment.'

'Me neither.'

They climbed over a stile, a long path ahead of them that meandered through the fields. The warm breeze shimmered across the corn, and when she put her arm around his waist, Josh swept her into a long slow dance.

* * * * *

*If you missed the previous story in the
Miracle Medics duet, then check out*

How to Heal the Surgeon's Heart
by Ann McIntosh

*If you enjoyed this story, check out these
other great reads from Annie Claydon*

**The Doctor's Reunion to Remember
Falling for the Brooding Doc
Greek Island Fling to Forever**

All available now!